Praise for Tawny Taylor's *Prince of Fire*

"Make certain to turn up the AC, have a cold drink and be prepared to have your breath taken away."

~ *Romance Junkies*

"...an exciting and engaging tale that will tug on your heart-strings and give you a little something to think about."

~ *The Romance Studio*

Look for these titles by
Tawny Taylor

Now Available:

Behind the Mask
Dirty Little Lies

Black Phoenix Series
Prince of Fire (Book 1)

Prince of Fire

Tawny Taylor

A SAṁhAIN PUϐLIShING, LτϽ. publication.

Samhain Publishing, Ltd.
577 Mulberry Street, Suite 1520
Macon, GA 31201
www.samhainpublishing.com

Prince of Fire
Copyright © 2009 by Tawny Taylor
Print ISBN: 978-1-60504-447-7
Digital ISBN: 978-1-60504-390-6

Editing by Anne Scott
Cover by Scott Carpenter

First Samhain Publishing, Ltd. electronic publication: February 2009
First Samhain Publishing, Ltd. print publication: December 2009

Dedication

To my family. I love you very much.

Chapter One

Talen Jacek was tall, dark and delicious, with a face that haunted Keri Maddox's dreams...and a body that inspired her fantasies.

He stood in her kitchen, glaring at her Mr. Coffee. The only barrier between her feasting eyes and his scrumptious body was a snowy cotton towel slung low on his hips. Outside of a large jagged scar that cut diagonally across his chest, he was a study in male perfection. Somehow, that one imperfection made him that much more stunning. It made him look *dangerous*.

Tiny droplets of water glistened on his wide, suntanned shoulders and smooth-skinned chest, and his dark, wavy hair was a riot of damp curls. Her fingers just itched to slide through their tangled, sexy thickness, to trace the intricate lines of the amazing black and grey tattoo of a bird, spread wings stretched from one side of his upper back to the other.

It was a sight straight out of last night's fantasy.

The only problem was, Talen was in the wrong apartment.

Keri knew for a fact that she'd locked her door this

morning when she'd left for work, and Talen didn't have a key. Talen didn't have a key because they weren't dating. They weren't roommates. They weren't even friends. Heck, they'd exchanged nothing but polite small talk since Talen had moved into the building. Granted, they'd exchanged more than their share of heated looks.

Sadly, he'd never made his move.

"Uh, hello?" Unable to stop from openly ogling her almost-naked neighbor, Keri dropped her purse on the counter. "What are you doing in my apartment, besides the obvious—abusing my coffeemaker?"

Talen glanced up, his expression shifted from nondomestic male confusion to beaming heartbreaker on-the-prowl. Keri caught the edge of the counter to steady herself.

"Hi. Sorry. I had a little accident." He motioned to the stove, which was coated with some sort of red substance—funny, she hadn't noticed that disaster before now. "I was trying to make spaghetti but the sauce sort of...burped all over me. So I jumped in the shower. I'm afraid I'm not exactly the King of Domesticity."

What gave Talen the idea that she'd expected him to be anything but the silent and mysterious neighbor with the adorable dimples?

"Ooookay." She went to the coffeemaker and started it. Oddly, she felt like she might need some hefty doses of caffeine tonight. She normally cut off all caffeine after six. Her body tingled all over when she shuffled past the mostly unclothed Talen, heading to the sink to arm herself with a wet sponge and some spray cleaner for the stove. She dumped the pot of soggy noodles she found in the sink before heading back to the stove. Once she checked the burners, making sure they were cool, she doused the entire stovetop in cleaner. "I'm afraid you've lost me. So, how about you start from the very beginning, like when you decided you needed to break into my apartment—"

"Oh, I didn't break in. The other guy did."

Huh? "What other guy? Where?" Suddenly realizing there might be a reason to be concerned about Talen's unexpected visit, she glanced around her kitchen.

She hadn't noticed anything odd when she'd first entered her apartment. Her door had been locked. The door itself had shown no obvious signs of a break-in, nothing to catch her attention. Her living room had been in its usual tidy state. The only thing out of the ordinary had been Talen.

Then again, maybe she'd been too distracted by his yummy self to notice anything else. Heck, she'd totally missed the mess on the stove until he'd pointed it out.

"You're telling me someone broke in? Like a burglar?" She swung around and checked the sliding door to her tiny balcony, wondering if the suspected burglar had come in that way. Unlikely as that was, since she lived on the second floor, she supposed it was possible.

"I'm guessing it was a burglar, although I'm not absolutely sure..."

The balcony door was shut, the curtains undisturbed.

Pivoting again, she glanced at Talen. "Someone was really in my apartment? How do you know?"

"Because...I heard something, a noise. Thud. No, a thump. And when I came to check, thinking you might've fallen, the door was hanging wide open."

"That's strange. A loud noise? Nothing seems to be knocked down. I wonder why anyone would break in..." Forgetting for a moment about her nearly naked guest, she hurried toward her bedroom, the room that was closest to Talen's apartment.

"I didn't see any sign of damage to the door or forced entry. But I did find something. Does this look familiar?" Behind her, Talen extended his arm, unfurling his fingers.

A gold cufflink.

A very unique and memorable cufflink.

Oh no. "Where?" The air left her lungs in a huff, and she staggered backward on shaky legs. Her hands flew to her face as she struggled to gulp in some much-needed air. Her stomach twisted in her belly. *No, no, no!*

"Keri?" Talen caught her upper arms and jerked her against him, wrapping her in a protective embrace. "What's wrong?"

Immediately, the awful nausea in her belly eased.

Mark Hayward, Esq. had taken their so-called breakup pretty badly, and after he'd showed up one night drunk and belligerent, she'd even filed for a personal protection order against him. Her application had been dismissed by the judge, but her threat to try again seemed to work when he showed up drunk a few nights later. He'd left her alone for a couple months. Until now.

Obviously, the spoiled-rich-kid-turned-attorney-slash-party-boy decided she wouldn't go through with the PPO, or maybe he knew it would be denied.

Darn it, she'd hoped he'd finally moved on, found someone else to obsess over. Stalk. He was a freaking lawyer. Who would've thought a guy with an impeccable reputation, a thriving law practice and more money than he could spend in ten lifetimes would be such a nutcase when it came to women?

What made things more confusing was the fact that they'd never officially been a *couple*. They'd only dated casually for a few weeks. And that was months ago.

"I'm okay. Honest...I think." She wriggled free from Talen's protective hold and headed toward her door. "That cufflink you found belongs to a guy I dated a while back. How'd he get in? Did you see him?"

"I think I missed him by seconds. The elevator door shut just as I came around the corner. I got only a glimpse of a guy with dark hair, shorter than me. Dark complexion."

"That's Mark."

"Mmmm, if you're not dating him anymore, you might want to get your key back."

"Key? I don't know how he'd get my key. I never gave him one. We were never that serious. And I haven't talked to him in months. Ohmygosh, I need to get the locks changed." She twisted the deadbolt and walked in a circle, not sure what to do first.

Talen stood silent, tracking her movement back and forth with his eyes. "I don't think you should stay here tonight."

"Great, now what?" She couldn't think, couldn't prioritize. What should she do first, call the apartment's office to request a new lock or go pack some stuff? Where would she stay? The thought of camping in some stupid hotel made her insides twist into knots.

This was insane—having to run from her home, to leave everything she owned and go into hiding because of one insane man who didn't know how to deal with rejection.

Would he just get over it already? Sheesh, she'd hate to see how he reacted when an honest-to-god girlfriend dumped him.

A part of her bristled at the notion that she'd have to let him basically bully her out of her own home, even temporarily. But the other part of her—the one that wasn't sure how demented he was—reminded her that being safe always trumped making a point. She'd watched enough of those true crime shows on television to know that a guy like this could be capable of some really horrific things.

Multitasking, she went for the cordless phone, punching the numbers for the apartment complex's office while hurrying around her bedroom. As she waited for someone to answer, she started tossing clothes into an overnight bag then rushed to the bathroom to gather some essentials.

After about twenty rings, she glanced at the clock.

Just freaking great. It was after six. The office was closed until tomorrow.

Talen was still standing in the kitchen, in her bath towel, when she returned from the bedroom. He poured a cup of freshly brewed coffee and handed it to her. "Want to tell me what's going on? Maybe I can help somehow."

"Oh, I don't want to drag you into my troubles. Like I said, the cufflink belongs to a guy I...dated casually—emphasis on casually—for a short time. Short, as in a couple of weeks. Clearly, he has issues with rejection. Unfortunately, he's not only the sole son of our governor but also a well-known lawyer with a brilliant future in politics ahead of him. No one wants to believe me when I say he's stalking me. Not even the police." She plucked the piece of jewelry from where Talen had left it on her kitchen counter and stuffed it into her pocket.

"Where are you going?" he asked.

"To the police station. Again. And then...I don't know." She sagged against a bar stool, dropping the overnight bag on the floor at her feet. "I guess I'll stay in a hotel until I can get the locks changed. This sucks. Why's he doing this? There's nothing here he could want. And it's not like what we had was all that great." Her cheeks warmed as Talen's brows knitted in surprise. "What I mean is, there are plenty of other women out there who don't mind a guy who's a bit on the controlling side. He's rich. Good looking. Me, I'd rather not deal with it, regardless of the size of his investment portfolio."

Talen nodded. "Got it." He kicked a foot over the other and leaned into the counter. "I have an idea. Just hear me out. You should stay with me instead of going to a hotel. That way you could come to your place and get what you need when you want, and you won't be alone—which is probably not safe, no matter where you stay. Plus, we can keep an eye on the place, maybe catch him in the act, so he'll be arrested or at least you'll be able to get that PPO."

That sounded like a good plan. A brilliant one, actually. The fact that she'd be staying with Talen, who had at least thirty pounds on her psycho-stalking lawyer, as well as a good four inches, made the idea all the more tempting. And even better, it would give her a chance to get to know this charming man with the dimples, enormous tattoo that spanned his back from shoulder to ass, and to-die-for body. Mmmm, he was something to look at.

"Are you sure?" she asked.

"Positive."

"I mean, this is asking a lot. What if stalker-lawyer-guy finds out I'm staying with you? He could come down and start giving you trouble too."

"Believe me, I know how to deal with guys like him. I can handle it."

She wanted to believe him, boy did she ever. "Can I ask, since we've hardly spoken before today, are you married? I'm not going to get in the way, am I?"

He shook his head. "Nope. Not married..."

Yeah!

He crossed his thick arms over his chest and leaned a hip against the counter. "And you won't be in my way. So, do you have everything you need?"

She took a second to glance around, but her mind wasn't focused. "Can I ask, what do you do? I'm not going to get you into trouble or anything, am I?"

"Not at all. I'm in the...security field. Personal security."

"You mean, like a bodyguard?" This was too much of a coincidence to believe. Her nerves started twitching.

"Yeah, like a bodyguard. I protect people, individuals. And at the moment I'm between jobs..."

Another coincidence.

The phone started ringing, yanking her attention to the handset sitting on the counter. She lifted it, glancing at the caller-ID display.

Mark's number. Ack!

Her heart literally stopped beating for a second.

Now what? Stay with the bodyguard, who just happened to be gorgeous, single and between jobs when she needed his services? Or take her chances on her own?

Her eyes jerked back to Talen.

Merely standing there, he gave off this dangerous, predatory vibe while still, somehow, making her feel safe and protected.

He smiled.

Her body proclaimed its choice.

The phone rang again, and a shiver of anticipation

17

skittered up her spine. She snatched up the phone, hoping Mark would explain everything and then she wouldn't have to go anywhere.

But there was a click and the call ended.

A second later, the phone rang again, and hopeful the first call had been cut short because of a bad connection, she answered, "Hello? Mark?"

This time, he said nothing. Only breathed.

Creepy! She hung up.

The phone rang again, and she threw her hands into the air. How could she think logically with so much going on? "Fine. I'll stay with you. But only on one condition—I pay the same price for your services as every other client would."

"I'm good with that if you are." He offered his hand.

She took it, and yet another zing of energy zapped up her arm. Her cheeks heated and she dropped her gaze to his navel. It had to be one of the sexiest belly buttons she'd ever seen. And of course it was situated dead center on one of the sexiest bellies she'd ever seen too. He had to have noticed she was gawking by now. Searching for safer territory, she snapped her head to the side and stared out the window instead. "Ooookay then."

A quick shake of his hand, and the deal was sealed.

A few bits of her anatomy did a happy dance.

"So, have you worked for anyone famous?" It had taken a few hours, and a fruitless trip to the police station—they still didn't believe her!—before Keri was finally starting to feel a smidge more comfortable with her new fulltime bodyguard. The fact that Talen was finally semiclothed helped a bit.

Wearing a pair of shorts and a snug black tank shirt that showed off his chest and shoulders to perfection, he lay sprawled on his very masculine black leather couch, the remote control in one fist, a can of cola in the other. Your typical guy. King of his castle.

She sat on the matching loveseat, her legs curled beneath her, a pillow propping her back and a coverlet thrown over her legs. Her head was mere inches from his, thanks to the relative position of the couch to the love seat. Definitely close enough to get a good look at that stunning face of his.

Cozy, her stomach full of Italian takeout and a couple of glasses of white wine, she was feeling better about things by the minute. Who knew? Maybe Mark had done her a favor tonight by pulling the stalker act. If he hadn't, Talen might have never gotten over his shyness or whatever it was that had kept him from saying more than "hey" when they passed in the hallway.

He took a swig from his can then set it on the coffee table with a clunk. "Yeah, you could call a few of them famous, I guess."

"Cool." She leaned closer. "Like who?"

His eyes twinkled as he shook his head, his lips

quirking into a smile that hinted at lots of secrets. "Can't tell you. It's in my contract."

"Even if you're not working for them anymore?"

"Yep." In the next several heartbeats of silence that followed, his gaze wandered over her face, making her a little squirmy, but in a good way.

She wondered if there was anything in the contract that forbade him from kissing her. He licked his lips, and her gaze lingered on the slick path his tongue had left behind.

"Have you been anywhere interesting?" she heard herself ask. How the heck had she managed to string together so many words in a row?

"Yes, I have. I've traveled all over Europe, Asia, Africa..."

Was it her, or was the heat cranked up to ninety? She pushed the coverlet off her lap and smoothed her hair into a ponytail, lifting it off her shoulders.

Twisting to face her, Talen tilted his head and reached, gathering the column of hair in his hands, and she knew, without a doubt, that he was going to kiss her.

Any second now.

He inched closer and she held her breath.

Her eyelids shuttered closed, and a comforting blackness cut off her sight, allowing her other senses to amplify. She could hear the soft, steady whoosh of his breathing. And the nerves in her neck and shoulders jangled from the fleeting touch of his knuckles as they scraped across her nape.

"You're beautiful." He was so close that his words fell like puffs of sweet-scented air on her mouth. "Do you know how many times I've wanted to do this...?"

"Do what?" she whispered, fully intending the words to be an invitation. Hot and tight, her body reacted to the sensations raining upon it like a spring shower—the erotic hunger she heard in his voice, the scent of his skin, the almost cruelly soft way he held her hair. She licked her lips, tasting the lingering flavor of wine. His mouth gently caressed hers, and she sagged against the loveseat's arm, drowning in sensual heat.

His fingers splayed, supporting the back of her head. He traced the seam of her mouth with his tongue, not exactly begging entrance but more or less making his intentions clear.

She eagerly opened, welcoming the sweet invasion. His tongue swept into her mouth, gliding over hers, a show of raw male possession. The fingers holding her head gently kneaded her scalp as his tongue and lips worked magic.

A kiss had never been so devastating. Her mind—usually delighted to scream all kinds of shoulds and shouldn'ts—went totally silent.

Wherever this was going, she wasn't about to fight it.

He broke the kiss for an agonizing second or two. "Damn, you taste good." He stood, walked around the end of the couch and paced back and forth once, twice, a third time. His head down, he shoved his fingers through his

21

hair. "Dammit."

"Is something wrong?"

His eyes found hers. "Yes. No." He charged toward her, caging her shoulders between his outstretched arms. "You taste so sweet, like honey. I want more."

A soft moan slipped between her lips, and a tremor raced up her spine. "Yes, more," she pleaded, relinquishing to the desire swirling through her. "Kiss me again." Oh, how beautiful he made her feel as he looked down upon her with flames flickering in his dark eyes. Pretty but also vulnerable and overpowered. It was a thrilling combination.

He climbed overtop of her, wedging one knee between her hip and the back of the loveseat and balancing the other one on the edge of the cushion. Bending his arms, he levered lower, until the heat radiating from his bulk warmed her simmering body and his mouth hovered over hers again. She closed her eyes and let her entire being focus on the place where his mouth met hers, and their tongues mated.

With every stab and stroke, the warmth in her body edged up another degree and the tension coiling deep in her belly knotted tighter. And yet she couldn't stop, couldn't stand the thought of tearing her mouth from his, even if it meant she'd burn up from fever or die from heart failure.

Never had she been kissed by a man like this, so incredibly strong and striking.

Dizzy. Hot.

She reached up and looped her arms around his neck, pulling him down, anxious to feel his hard body pressed firmly against hers, his hips wedged between her spread thighs.

A pounding ache was gathering there, in her center, and she rocked her hips, desperate to grind it away, hoping he wouldn't deny her the pleasure his kisses were promising.

Another sensual brush of his mouth across hers and then he straightened up, pulling her with him until she was sitting completely vertically, and his bent legs were straddling her tight and trembling thighs.

She watched, breathless, as he swallowed and smiled down at her.

He shook his head and dragged his fingers through his hair. "I'm sorry."

Oh God, he was apologizing. That was the last thing she wanted. It had been such a long time since a man had looked at her like that—like she was a desirable, sexy woman. Since a man had touched her. Talked to her with a voice gritty with barely contained wanting.

"I'm not sorry," she stated matter-of-factly. Her heart lurched in her chest when she realized she was going to actually admit she'd been attracted to him all this time. Guys didn't like to hear stuff like that. Her words just might send him running.

She knew a woman on the hunt tended to do that to men—turn them into skittery cowards. She'd watched her mother chase away enough good guys to have learned that lesson early. They liked things to go the other way. She did too. But for some reason, she sensed Talen needed to know she was okay with this, that she held no expectations other than those promised in his touches and kisses.

"I noticed you the very first day you moved into the building," she whispered. "I've waited, hoping, wanting..." Oh God, she sounded so sappy. "Not that I'm expecting anything. But I wanted you to know I don't feel taken advantage of here. Okay? I'm not letting this happen because I'm feeling scared or vulnerable right now. I've wanted this—whatever *this* might be—for a while. Because I think you're the most intriguing man I've ever met."

He cupped her cheek and ran his thumb over her lip, and she stared up into his eyes, wishing she could read whatever secrets she saw in their shadowed depths. She knew he was struggling with something and wished she could find the right words to put whatever inner battle he was waging to rest.

Talen shifted backward, simultaneously swinging off the loveseat. Shaking his head, he reached down and plucked one of Keri's delicate little hands up in his. This was so wrong, letting himself succumb to his desire for the angelic woman he'd been charged to protect. If he let things continue, the end would be disastrous.

If only...

"There are so many things about me you don't know,"

he said, pulling her to her feet.

To bed. That was where he needed to take her. He needed to put her in bed and leave, close the door, and walk away. Even if it meant he'd spend the rest of the night pacing the floor from the torment racking his body.

Keri was different than the others. He couldn't say what it was about her, but he felt something when she was near. A sense of...completion. Of peace and calm. In his long and anguish-riddled life, he'd had so few moments of peace, it was foreign to him, almost uncomfortable.

Why Keri? Why now?

The end was near. He felt it move closer with every second that ticked by. Soon, he'd face that moment, when it would be either her life or his, and the darkness would take him, and for a brief instant he'd be free. Until the blaze engulfed him in agony once again, and he was set back upon the earth to do it all over.

Live, die, regenerate. It was a cycle he was powerless to escape. His destiny. His curse. And his blessing.

He was the legendary Black Phoenix, a prince who had been cursed by the gods for having been too blinded by lust to make the right choice when it mattered most. Now, thanks to that curse, he would forever burn with lust. Because he could never experience true love, the profound joy of giving his heart to a woman.

There was no time. His cycle in any one place was so brief, weeks at the most. And even if there was time to get to know a woman, to do so would mean her certain destruction. No woman deserved to watch the man she loved lay down his life. Not if it could be avoided.

He'd tried to slake his baser needs once. But the results...the woman had killed herself after watching him die. The tragedy had taught him a painful lesson. His future would be an eternity of isolation and loneliness. A hell he couldn't have imagined when he'd first been cursed.

The only comfort he took was in knowing he would save a life every time he regenerated. Just like now. Keri would live...because he would die.

Chapter Two

Keri stood at the door, the knob in her fist, confused and torn. The sensible part of her knew it was pretty damn stupid leaving Talen's safe apartment to return to her own. *If* she was in any real danger, that was.

But another part—the one ruled by emotion—couldn't stand the thought of staying in this place another minute. Everything here was like a painful reminder of the firm, albeit gentle, rebuff he'd given her.

Rejection sucked.

So what if she didn't know all his deep, dark secrets? Why should that keep a man from enjoying a little carnal pleasure? She wasn't a prude. She wasn't a slut either, but she didn't have to know a guy's life story before she had sex with him. Heck, when things were just getting started, a bit of mystery was good. It made her feel tingly and warm all over. Especially with a man like Talen, who emitted this kind of darkly predatory aura she found so sexy.

She'd be the first to admit, she tended to attract players. That was because of her fascination with men who were distant and closed off, strong and unattainable.

One of her friends had tried to tell her she was actually playing it safe, going after men like that.

She probably was.

Of course, she didn't explain to said friend that life had taught her the kind of vulnerability that came with true love was too scary and dangerous. She wasn't ready to go there yet. Might never be.

Now what? Let her ego get the best of her and leave, facing an uncertain danger? Or stay there and be a houseguest to a man with a body that made her weak in the knees...and a conscience that made her want to beg?

Well, darn it, did she really know for a fact that Mark was out to harm her? Maybe he'd just broken in to get something he'd thought he'd left behind? What that might be, she had no clue. They hadn't spent any length of time in her apartment during the few dates they'd shared.

Mark? Dangerous? Was her imagination running amok, making her think the worst?

He'd stalked her. There was no denying that. He'd harassed her, begged her to take him back. But he'd never directly threatened to harm her. Nor had he behaved in a brutal or openly aggressive manner. Which was why she hadn't been able to get a judge to grant a PPO. There'd been no threats. No violence. Just annoyances, which were evidently not against the law.

Leave it to an attorney to know exactly how to tiptoe along that fine line between legal and illegal.

She released the doorknob and slumped back on the bed. She needed to think logically here. First, she was ninety-nine percent sure the man who had let himself into her place was Mark. He hadn't damaged or stolen anything. Chances were he wasn't up to something sinister, just annoying. If he had a criminal record, she had to trust that the police would've told her, or the judge would have approved the PPO.

This was silly. She'd let her imagination run wild.

If she was in no real danger, she didn't need a bodyguard. Especially one who was messing with her head by sending mixed signals.

She threw her overnight bag over her shoulder and headed for the door again, this time certain she was doing the right thing. Mark didn't deserve to be given so much power over her life, and Talen didn't need to be put out by an unwanted guest.

Talen jackknifed up, instantly alert, his senses sharp.

The killer was close. Too close.

Keri?

He launched himself from the couch and ran to the bedroom.

Empty. Dammit.

He rubbed at the burning skin at his nape, the friction only inflaming the scorching sensation. It was time, already. He'd had very few hours with her. To think it had to end so soon. He'd come to her the minute he'd learned of her identity.

The gods were cruel. They'd waited until practically

the last minute before revealing her identity to him.

He'd never learn what secrets she hid in those shadowed eyes of hers, what made her laugh, or even what her favorite food was...

Unless... He hadn't tried delaying the inevitable. Testing fate. Defying the gods.

Hurry.

He spun around and bolted across his apartment, focused on the door. Out he went, into the corridor. Silently, he crept down the hallway.

Her door was ajar, and he could hear scuffling noises, struggling, Keri's muffled voice.

No. Dammit! It was too late. He wouldn't be able to halt the chain of events now.

His heart in his throat, he peered through the gap between the door and frame, catching sight of her assailant, the flash of a large blade, and her little struggling form. Without thinking, he shoved open the door and threw himself at Keri's captor, who pivoted, calmly, coolly, and placed a hunting knife across Keri's throat.

"Get. Out," the attacker growled.

Keri's tear-filled eyes met Talen's, and for an agonizing moment, he prayed he'd somehow make it out of this one alive, even if it meant he'd die tomorrow anyway.

Just one more day with her, hearing her voice, looking at her face. One more day to make things right. To try to explain why he'd rejected her last night.

Shit, it was too soon.

He'd been cheated out of the chance to tell her how he felt. It wasn't the first time. It wouldn't be the last either. His curse made sure he would never have the chance to love another human being again. He'd known that a long while, even come to accept it. But with this woman, his Keri, it was a hundred times more agonizing.

No, goddammit. He was being selfish. Keri didn't need to understand him. Or care. She needed to survive and move on.

The attacker's fingers tightened on the knife's handle. "I said, get the hell out."

The guy didn't want to kill Keri. Talen could see the hesitation in his eyes. Of course, he was destined to. Today. Now. Talen decided to use the attacker's uncertainty to his advantage.

Talen met the man's glare. "No."

Stalemate.

Keri's eyes narrowed slightly, and her body went rigid then soft. Talen could read the subtle changes in her posture. The attacker could feel them too. He glanced down, and that was all the time Talen needed. He lunged forward at the same instant that Keri's body slipped from the attacker's grip.

The knife surged forward, and Talen braced himself for the pain. This was it, the end. There'd be the physical agony. But that was nothing compared to the hell of being yet again yanked away from someone who knew his name, recognized the fact that he existed.

A heartbeat later, the pain still hadn't come. Shaking himself out of a daze, Talen realized the attacker had knocked Keri unconscious with a fist, the other one, still gripping the knife, was rising to deliver a final, deadly blow.

He saw red.

Talen threw himself at the assailant, his target the knife. He twisted mid-air, diving between the weapon and Keri's still body. He landed on top of her, his vision locked on the gleaming tip of the blade as it made its descent.

His heart lurched.

He'd be dead in a few seconds, and Keri would never know...

No! Have mercy.

Instead of taking the blade in his chest and ending it like he should, Talen threw himself away, pulling Keri with him, and plowing into the side of the armed man's leg. A sickening snap filled the tense silence and the attacker stumbled then lurched toward the door. Desperate to capture the would-be killer, Talen jerked around but he toppled over a fallen lamp before he got his feet beneath him. The man staggered out the door and was down the hall before Talen could get vertical.

Now what had he done?

Angered the gods, for one. Who knew what would happen next.

If he'd died, Keri's attacker would've died with him,

somehow, whether it was by an injury Talen had caused in the battle or a seeming act-of-fate. That was the way the magic worked. Instead, the attacker was still alive, and plotting his next move.

The danger wasn't over. Keri's suffering not even close to being finished.

His fault.

Swamped in guilt, Talen knelt beside Keri and gazed down at her face. She looked like she was sleeping. Eyes closed. Glossy hair fanned around her head like a glittering halo. Expression peaceful.

The peace would end the moment she regained consciousness. And the nightmare would begin.

His fault.

He'd been weak, and look what it would cost them both.

For the first time in over two thousand years, he wept.

It took several minutes for Keri to fully wake up and remember what had happened.

Oh my God, it had been like a scene straight out of a Lifetime movie! She'd just gone to bed when she'd heard a noise. The next thing she knew, a strange man was standing next to her bed, saying things she didn't understand.

She'd run. Made it as far as the living room. He'd caught her. Talen came bursting into her apartment. Right about then, she'd started seeing stars, thanks to the terror. And her head felt like it had exploded. The rest was hazy. But not forgotten.

A nightmare had woken her up.

Bathed in sweat and gasping, she threw off the covers and lurched forward. "Where am I?"

"It's okay. You're safe. I brought you back to my place." Talen appeared out of the thick darkness and immediately pulled her into his arms. She stiffened for a split second, unable to help herself. But the edge of her terror softened by his steady strength and warmth, she relaxed against him.

She wanted to thank him, but her throat was closed up too tightly and her teeth chattered. All that escaped was an occasional stifled sob. She tried to control the quaking but couldn't. She felt like she couldn't breathe, that the air wasn't getting into her lungs fast enough. Her head started spinning again as the horrifying scene in her apartment played over and over in her mind.

He held her tenderly, smoothing a hand up and down her back. A simple gesture but so appreciated. He said nothing, just held her. Finally, after who knew how long, the spinning slowed. The air moved in and out of her lungs easier. The shuddering eased.

She tipped her head to look at his face.

His lips were pulled into a thin line, his eyes dark.

"It wasn't who I thought," she whispered.

"Who?"

She shivered. "The man who attacked me. I didn't

know him. What's going on?"

Talen's mouth thinned even more. "I'll find out."

"We should call the police."

"I'll take care of it, while you rest."

She wanted to call now, get it over with, while the memories of the man's face were still fresh, but she had a feeling it wouldn't be a short conversation. Quite the opposite.

She glanced around, found a clock. It was just after three. She'd only been sleeping for a couple of hours.

Her head hurt.

She was tired. And still shaking.

She rubbed at her temples. "You'll call the police?"

"Yes, in a few minutes." Talen eased beneath the covers beside her and, taking her with him, lay on his back, cradling her head. He tucked her against him, until she lay flush to his side. Despite the pounding in her head, a current of sensual awareness rippled through her body.

So big. And brave. And strong.

She'd been an absolute idiot for leaving his apartment earlier. Granted, she'd had absolutely no clue how much danger she was in. But to think her stung pride had almost cost her life...and worse, Talen his. She'd never be able to live with the guilt if he'd been hurt, let alone killed.

Tears burned her eyes. "Dammit, if I wasn't so freaked out and exhausted, I might handle this better." Mad at herself for crying, she dragged the back of her hand across her eyes. She sniffled. "I'm sorry I left."

He caught her chin and forced her to meet his gaze. Gently, he wiped a tear from her cheek. "You don't have to apologize. I'm the one who should be saying I'm sorry."

"Why? What do you mean? If I hadn't gone back to my place, the attacker wouldn't have found me, and you wouldn't have practically gotten stabbed to death."

"And if I hadn't kissed you..." He pulled her tighter to his side.

The tiny ripples inside her started getting bigger.

Great, now she was horny, on top of mad...and scared...and confused. God help her, she wanted him to make her forget. For a while. "I liked the kiss. I wanted more."

He nuzzled her hair. "So did I."

"Then why stop?" She smoothed a hand over his chest, mapping the line of the scar beneath his T-shirt. "I wasn't complaining."

He caught her hand just as a fingertip found a hard nipple. His fingers clamped around her wrist like a vise. Rolling, he dragged her arm over her head and pinned her body beneath his.

Ooooh, yes. She'd just pushed a button, a pretty lethal one, at that. For some crazy reason, the terror of the earlier attack made the physical contact with Talen that much more powerful. No, *essential*.

She needed his touch, desperately. She needed to know she was alive. To be certain someone realized she existed. To feel another human being's hands on her body, arms locked around her waist.

Staring up into eyes that had gone dark and wild, she dragged in a deep breath. Above her was a man on the verge of losing control.

She was in heaven.

His heartbeat pounded so hard and fast she could feel it thumping against her breasts. And his breaths were so quick and shallow they puffed like soft gusts over her face. Her heart started racing too.

"I don't know what it is about you," he whispered, his gaze jumping from her eyes to her mouth and then back to her eyes again.

"I'll take that as a compliment." The heat swelling in her body was making her feel squirmy.

Pulsing. Thrumming. Liquid heat.

"It's been so long since I've touched a woman like this, since I've dared. Or since anyone has touched me."

His words shocked her, and the hollow tone of his voice left her feeling empty. Yet the throbbing need swelling inside her didn't ease. In fact, it increased until her face flamed.

This man had more than a few secrets. He had lots of them, and God help her, she wanted to know every one.

"Touch me, Talen. Please. I'm begging."

A long stretch of silence dragged between them, only somewhat softened by the sounds of their shallow breathing. It was agony and ecstasy both. To be so close and yet have him refuse to lay his hands on her.

"Talen?"

"Oh, may the gods forgive me."

Talen's kiss was nothing like earlier. It was a hard, hungry possession. Tongue, teeth, lips. He tasted and took, conquered and seduced.

Suddenly finding both arms pinned over her head, she returned every stroke and stab, every sigh and moan.

The pounding ache between her legs intensified once again as flames of desire danced and twisted in her chest. She dragged her feet apart, allowing Talen's hips to nestle between her thighs. More sweet torture.

God yes, this was so good, so right. Talen was everything she'd ever wanted in a lover. Strong and powerful, sensual and attentive, a little mysterious. And also, in a strange and unexpected way, vulnerable.

She had no idea what it would take to keep him around after all this craziness was over, but somehow she'd do it. This man, she wanted for more than a night or two. By revealing his weakness, by allowing her to see how desperately he wanted her, he had done what so many others had failed to do.

He had already left a tiny mark on her heart.

Burning up. So hot.

Too much material between them, a torturous barrier.

A whimper bubbled up from deep inside, slipped between her lips, to be swallowed up by Talen.

How much longer would he torment her like this?

Cruel bastard!

She dragged her mouth from his, jerking her head to the side. It took several hard gasps to pull enough air in her lungs to speak. "Talen, clothes."

Eyes glassy, face flushed, hair mussed, he nodded, crossed his arms and lifted his shirt over his head, revealing abs straight out of a fitness magazine. Up her gaze went, following the bottom of his shirt, from a washboard stomach to tight pecs, broad chest, glorious face.

While his hands were occupied, she set hers to work too, working the button of his fly. Pop, out it came, down went the zipper, revealing a vee of smooth-skinned flesh. No underwear. God, that was sexy!

She glanced up, her gaze catching a look of carnal need on Talen's face and her blood began to boil. He pushed her onto her back, practically tore her shirt and bra off, and yanked her pants off, leaving nothing between her quivering body and his scorching hot gaze but one unsubstantial pair of lace panties.

"Don't move," he growled, his jaw set. He rolled off her and shoved his pants down, revealing a thick, full erection, a set of heavily muscled legs, and...oh yes, he was turning around...that was one fine butt.

Her panties became even wetter.

Then, moving with the stealth and restrained power of a jungle cat, he climbed onto the bed. Over her. On hands and knees. His gaze raking across her exposed flesh so intensely it felt like a literal caress.

No, not a caress, it was a harder touch, like fingernails dragging against her skin, down from her collarbone, over the swell of both breasts. Her nipples pebbled, tight and hard.

She arched her back, pushing them higher, a silent plea for his touch. If only he'd take them into his warm mouth, suckle them.

"You are incredible, beautiful, perfect," he murmured, sounding almost awestruck. It was so touching and sweet, she nearly melted.

She wanted to tell him the many thoughts that were running through her head, but she was afraid to, knowing they'd ruin the moment. Instead, she bit her lip and gave him a grateful smile. When he didn't move or speak, she took his hand in hers and pulled it to her, flattening it over her breast.

He glanced askance, waiting for a nod before he gently fondled her soft fullness. Inside, she screamed, *more.* But outside, she kept her face a mask of absolute rapture, encouraging him with soft sighs and groans.

Oh so right. So good.

He pinched her nipple, rolled it, sending white-hot blades of desire shooting through her body.

"Yes, oh yes." She arched her back more, parted her quivering thighs. The burning ache between them pounded on and on, ever increasing, growing more urgent. Still, he continued a slow, meticulous torment. He pulled one turgid nipple into his mouth and finally slipped a hand between her legs to explore her center.

More desperate for release than ever before, she grabbed his head, fisted his hair, and pulled. Her hips rocked against his shy, teasing touch.

Harder. Please, harder.

Too empty.

The inner walls of her sex clamped around aching emptiness and wave after wave of liquid heat throbbed from them. A fingertip dipped inside, and she swore she was about to die.

Out it went and she swallowed a sob.

"Talen, you're cruel."

"I don't want it to end too quickly. Too fast." He sounded as breathless as she felt. His finger slipped inside her again, and this time, she clamped her inner muscles around it.

Ooooh...

"And you're tight," he murmured, testing her. "Sweet goddess."

Sweet goddess was right! Did he know what he was doing to her? What that fingertip was stroking?

A guttural sound rumbled from his chest, and she smiled, sensing he was as close to snapping as she was. Every cell in her body celebrated when he inched higher, licking, nipping and kissing his way up her torso, over her breasts to her neck, ears, chin, cheeks, mouth.

"Rubber?" she whispered.

"Rubber?" He tipped his head, giving her a puzzled, flush-faced look.

"You know, condom? If you don't have any, I have one. In my purse. Oh, wait. Do I have my purse?"

"Um. Yes, I brought your bag and purse, but no. I don't have a condom."

"I'll get one. Where did you put my things?" She started to get up, but he held her in place.

"No. I'll get it." He returned, her purse clasped in one strong hand, before she'd been able to catch her breath.

"My girlfriend stuck these in here when we went to the bar. Long story." She fished one out—Ultra Ribbed for her pleasure—and handed it to Talen.

He tore open the wrapper, unrolled the rubber, inspected it, and finally after much difficulty, put it on. Clearly, he had never used one before. She wasn't sure how to feel about that.

He settled his hips between her spread legs.

Soon! She'd be full of hard, hot cock. Finally, the flared tip of his rod nudged at her opening, and she opened her legs wider and held her breath.

Now, please now.

He inched inside, his shaft stretching her, a slow, absolutely exquisite invasion. Deeper, deeper still, until he had fully seated himself within her. They groaned in unison. Just as slowly, he withdrew, the intimate caress stirring the heat blazing in her body to near lethal temperatures.

In and out, he shafted her with the meticulous care he'd taken in every act of foreplay. She'd never had such an attentive, thorough lover. He seemed to be relishing every sensation—sight, taste, sound, touch—like it was his first time.

Surely, it couldn't be. Not with the skill he was showing, how he knew exactly where to touch her, how much pressure, to drive her wild with desire.

Angling back, he knelt upright and forced her legs wide apart. He found the hard nub nestled beneath the folds of her labia and stroked up and down. With every thrust of his rod, every caress of her clit, she soared closer to the pinnacle.

In moments, her skin was slick, her muscles trembling, and a whirling vortex of energy was gathering strength in her core. Seeming to sense her upward climb toward completion, he quickened the pace of his caresses. She could tell he was there too, with her. His deep breaths echoed in her head, a glorious accent to the soft slapping sound of their flesh meeting.

The scent of sex hung heavy and sweet in the air, and she gulped it in, eager to drink her fill. She swept her tongue over her lower lip then bit, tasting his kiss still lingering on her mouth.

Harder, faster his length drove in and out, and harder, faster her heartbeat and breathing became. She closed her eyes and let the sensations carry her away, to a beautiful place where she could see scents, taste colors, where her entire being was as small and tight as a pinhead, centered on the pleasure Talen's body was giving her.

One glorious second later that pinhead exploded in a huge blast of colors and heat. A wave of tingling, zapping bliss shot out from her center, blazing up to the roots of her hair and down to the soles of her feet. The spasms followed, as her body milked Talen's cock, drawing out her pleasure, making it last for an eternity. It was the most intense orgasm she had ever experienced, the longest too. It barely eased when her body tightened again, the heat of a second climax gathering in her core.

Talen pistoned into her, just the way her body demanded. She rocked her hips, taking him as deep as she could and moaned as a second orgasm rolled over her like a tidal wave. A flurry of sensations blasted her mind, and she opened her eyes, falling deep into Talen's hooded gaze. A low growl slipped past Talen's lips. He cupped her face, holding it tenderly as he found release. Hot air singed the skin of her chest and stomach.

The heat slowly eased.

Talen withdrew, disposed of the rubber, lay down and gathered her close.

She smiled as she rested her head on his chest, listening to the racing *thump-wump* of his heartbeat and the whoosh of air sawing in and out of his lungs. His skin smelled sweet and spicy.

Warm. Safe. Content. She'd be happy to stay like this forever.

Was there any chance this was really as magical and special as it seemed? They were virtual strangers and yet this felt good. Right. Perfect. Like they'd known each other for years, had made love every night, knew every inch of each other's bodies.

Could this man accomplish what so many others had failed to do? Or was she a fool for even hoping that might be true?

Chapter Three

Talen couldn't speak. He could barely look Keri in the eye. Not when she was looking at him like *that*. Oh, goddess. Now what?

He was a shit. The worst kind of scum. He'd been weak, and instead of resisting Keri as he should have, he'd let his defenses slip.

She was so beautiful and vulnerable. But those weren't the characteristics that had led him to do the unforgivable.

He'd met a lot of women over the centuries, many of them beautiful like Keri, and all of them vulnerable in some way too. What had made Keri different was that she'd warmed his icy heart somehow. It had been centuries since anyone had done that, so long he'd almost forgotten how good it felt.

Maybe it had been what he'd seen in her eyes as they'd shared the most intimate moments any two people could experience. Or perhaps it was the way her face lit when she smiled. He couldn't say. All he knew was that the ice encasing this prince of fire's heart had melted, releasing a flood of emotions he hadn't known he was capable of feeling again.

He was overjoyed and yet devastated. The price for these precious moments would be Keri's to pay, and that was almost enough to destroy him.

What if Keri took her own life, like Tanith had? When the gods had shown him what had happened, and the eternal price Tanith had paid for committing suicide, a part of his soul had crumbled to dust. The next time he was rejuvenated, he not only remembered everything about his condemned lover but he discovered he had a festering wound on his chest. And unlike the injuries he suffered with each death, it wasn't healed by the gods before he returned to the living. Instead, it remained. A punishment.

Slowly, it healed. It took many deaths and rebirths to notice. Years passed. Eons. Until finally the infection cleared. The burning eased. Still, even now, he bore a ragged, tight scar across from the base of his throat to the bottom of his ribcage. And his memories of her remained impossibly clear, right down to the anguish in her eyes as she watched him die. Painful reminders to keep his vow.

He couldn't let Keri suffer the same fate. It was that simple. Couldn't. Let. That. Happen...again.

"I don't normally do this." Keri wore nothing but a towel as she padded barefoot from the bathroom. Her long hair fell in heavy wet waves over her shoulders and down her back. Fat sparkling droplets of water dripped from the curled ends.

Unsure whether she was waiting for a response from

him or not, he nodded. "Me neither."

"I mean, I've had my share of casual sex..." Her cheeks and forehead flushed a hot pink that had him wishing he had a lot more time to spend with her, like years. "Oh God, I sound so pathetic." Plopping on the bed, she smacked her hands over her face. "I'm going to scare you away. I just know it."

If only there was some way he could stay with her. For one more day. He'd pay any price, make any sacrifice.

As long as that sacrifice was his to pay, not hers.

He thought he'd been to hell but Hades had nothing on the place he'd taken them to now. He sat beside her, drawing her onto his lap. He inhaled the scent clinging to her hair, dragging one deep breath after another. "You couldn't scare me away if you tried."

Her hands slid down her face, revealing a set of hope-filled eyes. "Really?" And he knew then and there that he needed to tell her everything.

This would be the first time for him. Telling his secret had been forbidden. But he would gladly face the wrath of every god in the heavens if it meant Keri would be able to go on with her life after he died.

"I need to tell you a story." He gently pried her fingers off her face and kissed her fingertips, each one. "About a man who was once very selfish and narrow-minded."

"Who was this man? Was it you?"

"It was. A long time ago, I did a terrible thing. I let my lust for a woman blind me to what was truly important. I've paid the price for my sin for many years, and it's time to pay again."

"What's that mean?" Her fist tightened around the bottom of her towel toga. Her head dropped. "Please, don't give me some convoluted explanation for why you won't see me anymore. I can't stand to hear one more illogical explanation from another man. You don't know what—"

"Look at me."

When she didn't lift her eyes, he cupped her chin and gave it a gentle nudge.

Slowly, her gaze climbed to his. She didn't say a word. She didn't have to. He could feel her pain, like a dull blade, sawing at his insides.

"I'm not making anything up. I'm trying to explain so that you'll understand what's about to happen. This is eating me up inside because it was my weakness that brought us here. And now I am utterly powerless to do anything to stop what's coming next."

"What's going to happen next, Talen?"

Silence.

How could he say it? How could he make her understand?

"I'm going to die," he stated.

Shock raced across her face then tightened her body.

As if she was searching for some sign, her gaze swept over his face down his body then climbed back up again. "Are you sick?"

"No. I'm..." Would she believe him? Probably not. But he still had to tell her the truth. He owed her at least that much. "Cursed. It's the price I must pay for my crime."

"Crime?" Her eyebrows sank over her eyes. "You're what, then? Going to be executed?"

"Not exactly."

"I don't understand." Her voice reflected all the confusion he saw in her eyes.

"Sometime later today the man who attempted to kill you will try again. And I will step in and stop him. But in doing so, I'll die."

"How can you be so sure that's the way things are going to happen?"

"Because it's my destiny. It's how it was supposed to happen earlier."

"Shit." Keri slid off his lap and rambled around the room, scooping up her clothes and lobbing them onto a chair. Then she hauled the bundle into the bathroom. When she came out, she was fully dressed. She stood next to the bathroom door, stared at him for several long moments. "This doesn't make any sense." Once again, she started hurrying around the room. Tidying clothes, making the bed, gathering her things.

Tracking her movements, he struggled against the need to capture her in his arms and soothe her. "It sounds like complete insanity to you. I realize that. But that doesn't make it any less true."

She stopped in the dead center of the room and stared at him for a heartbeat before jerking her gaze away. "Okay, did some psychic tell you this? Or are you perhaps a schizophrenic who forgot to take his medicine?"

Desperate to help her accept a truth she couldn't possibly understand, he jumped to his feet and caught her upper arms, forcing her to look at him. "Listen, sometimes you just have to believe things, even when they are illogical. Don't listen with your head. Listen with your heart."

Long moments stretched between them. The air felt hot and heavy, and currents of electricity leapt between their bodies, making him jittery.

And then the sickening feeling returned, and he knew the killer was nearby. His time with Keri was short. Somehow, he had to make her listen. He had to hear she'd forgiven him for what he'd done. He had to know she wouldn't do anything foolish after he died.

"Please, just tell me you'll forgive me. I wanted to be with you. Desperately...to hear your voice, and feel your touch. I defied the gods. And then when the chance came again, I refused to take the fatal blow. I needed some time to explain...I didn't even know if it was possible..."

"That's enough." Her eyes were cold, her voice clipped. She pulled away, shrugging out of his hold. He watched his fingers uncurl from around her arms. "You honestly believe this? Why was spending time with me that important, if it's going to cost you so much?"

He stared down at the floor, regret burning him up inside. What a bastard he was. She'd never believe him. Never. What had made him think she could? Let alone, be able to forgive him.

He slumped onto the bed and listened to the soft

rustle of cloth as she hurried around the room. Words drifted through his mind, and he just let them come. "Can you imagine what it feels like to be virtually invisible to everyone? To not exist?" He glanced up.

The sharp edge in her gaze softened somewhat. Her lips parted, her chest rose and fell several times, but she didn't speak for a long time. Finally, she whispered, "Maybe."

"Then we have that much in common."

"I guess we do. But it's my choice." Apparently running out of clutter to tidy, she plopped into the chair tucked in the corner of the room. She bent her knees, wedging her feet up tight against her bottom and wrapped her arms around her shins. "If you fly under the radar, no one expects anything from you. Right?"

"Sure. But why are you hiding?"

"Long story. Tell me yours."

He knew she didn't want to hear his, not really. She'd never believe it. But she'd been pushed into a corner, figuratively, and she was looking for an escape route.

She had no idea how grateful he was for the chance to tell his story, to feel like he mattered to someone, even if it was for such a short time. And even if she wasn't sure how to react to him.

All that mattered was she was here, with him, listening, talking, connecting. This was what his humanity craved, what he had been denied for so long.

"I've been living in this hellish place, a continual cycle of empty existence, loneliness, sacrifice, followed by suffering and resurrection. I get only a brief glimpse of peace before the cycle begins again. When I'm here, among the living, I stay in one place for only a short time. I can't afford to let anyone get close because I know what's coming next. It's not fair to them, to you. It'll hurt to watch me die."

Her gaze was probing, as she sat with her chin on her knees, arms hugging herself tightly. "But with me...?"

"I couldn't stop myself. That's why I've asked for your forgiveness. Because soon I'll die. For you. And you're going to grieve."

She paled. Her lips thinned.

"It was my choice to talk to you. To touch you. To kiss you and hold you, to let myself...exist...in your world, rather than just lay down my life and go on to the next one." He could hear his voice deepening with grief and regret.

"Not that I'm totally buying this, but what if you didn't...die?"

"It's either you or me. If I don't..." He honestly didn't know the answer to her question. What would happen? He'd never dared to challenge the will of the gods before now.

Too jittery to sit, he surged to his feet and headed to the window. Summer, fall, winter, spring, rainy, sunny, cold or warm. It didn't matter what the weather was outside. It never stayed the same for long, not for him. And yet, his hand went to the curtain. He pulled it back and peered out.

The sky was a crisp, clear blue but to the west, grey clouds hung low, fat and heavy with rain. The sun hunched low to the east yet. Morning.

Despite the uncertainty weighing so heavily on his shoulders, today was a good day to die. He shouldn't feel this way, but for once he was ready to face the moment when he'd leave this life. Because for once he wouldn't die alone, with nobody having realized he had even lived.

"It's ironic. So much has changed since I walked upon this earth as a mortal," he mused, watching the people below amble down the street, passing in and out of the buildings flanking either side of the road. "Yet human beings are still the same. They haven't changed much at all."

"How much has the world changed, Talen?" Her voice was closer.

Twisting, he glanced over his shoulder, surprised to see she was standing only a few feet behind him. Her arms were hugging her torso like they had been earlier, but the disbelief that had once pulled her pretty features into tight lines was all but gone. "I doubt you'd believe me if I told you."

"Could it be any more shocking than you telling me you are like some kind of human phoenix, living and dying over and over?"

"Maybe not, but it's interesting you compare me to the phoenix, because that's precisely what I am. Before I was cursed, I was the prince of a Phoenician city-state, a ruler who was known as the Prince of Fire or the Black

Phoenix. I'd never have guessed my name would one day be my curse.

"Over the millennia, I've watched war destroy millions of lives. A savior be born, slain and resurrected. A new church form in his name. Great civilizations crumble. Man battle man with machines, and now chemicals. Buildings rise from the ground, first made from the earth, then wood, metal, glass. Streets hewn into the countryside, widen and multiply, cutting the landscape into a patchwork of stripped forests and crowded cities..."

"So much." She sounded awestruck. "I mean, the 'savior' you mentioned, that was Jesus?"

"Yes."

She blinked, several times. "Really? The Son of God? Jesus?"

"Yes."

"You met him?"

"I did. Once."

She inched back, pushed her hands through her mussed hair, sending the deep brown waves cascading over her shoulders. "Uh...wow. That means you're more than two *thousand* years old."

"Yes, I am."

"I feel so...I don't know. This is beyond weird, actually talking to a human being who lived during the time of Jesus." Her gaze lurched away, and she spun around, wrapping those slender arms around herself again. Her steps faltered as she hurried back toward the chair in the corner. Turning, she stood in front of it, one hand braced against the back. "I've often looked at Mrs. Goodrich downstairs and imagined what kinds of changes she's witnessed in her lifetime. But you..."

He couldn't help smiling. "The lady in 1B."

"She looks ancient." A dark pink tint colored her cheeks. "I mean, for the average person, she looks pretty old. To you, her lifetime is like a..."

"A blink. And an eternity, both."

"Yeah." She straightened up, seeming to be able to stand on her own. She stared at the floor, lost in her thoughts.

Once more, a heavy silence dropped between them, pushing them apart. He sensed Keri's inner struggle, could see it in the confusion churning in her eyes like storm clouds when she lifted them.

Finally, she whispered, "What kind of gods would do something so cruel, Talen? Nobody deserves the kind of hell you've been dragged through."

"I don't blame the gods for my punishment. I blame myself. I was the one who committed the crime."

Something flashed in Keri's eyes again, something he couldn't read. She moved closer, and the air filled with the fresh, damp scent of her skin and hair. His body tightened at her nearness, blood surging through his veins, warming his skin. He ached to pull her against him and bury his nose in the crook of her neck. To taste her skin. To kiss her.

If only he could die with the flavor of her kiss still

clinging to his lips. What a great comfort that would be. But, in all truth, he didn't deserve any comfort, including that one. Especially now.

No doubt, the gods would be even crueler with this death. And the last one hadn't been painless, not by a long shot.

Tentatively, she lifted her fingers and extended her arms. When her fingertips grazed the backs of his hands, she looked into his eyes. "Do you know when it'll happen? When...?"

"I feel a burning sensation here." He rubbed the back of his neck, which was tingling, although the heat was slight. "The closer we get to that time, the more painful the sensation becomes."

As if she'd feel it too, she reached for his nape, fingering his warm skin. He looked down at her sweet face, determined to commit every miniscule detail of her features to his memory forever. Long, dark lashes. Sparkling blue eyes the same shade as the sky outside. Full lips that tasted sweet like a ripe peach. Faded freckles sprinkled over the bridge of her nose.

"Here?" she asked.

"Yes, there."

She tipped her head up to him. "How much longer do we have together?"

"A few hours, I'm guessing."

"That's all?" Her lips pursed into a slight pout. "So little time. What should we do?"

"I'm content to just stay here and talk...touch. What do you want?" He placed his hand against her cheek, relishing the satiny smooth texture of her skin. So warm. He felt a smile tugging at his lips.

"Will you do more than touch me on the face?" She rested her flattened hand against the back of his and then slowly pulled, dragging his palm down the side of her neck, over her collarbone, to her breast. "Maybe I'm not a zillion years old like you, but I've been lonely for a long time too. And maybe there's a reason why you're here with me now, instead of lying dead in my apartment. Maybe your gods aren't punishing you. Maybe they're rewarding us both. With a chance to have something neither of us has been able to accept in a long time. A connection with another human being."

Another emotion swirled in his gut, threatening to fill his eyes with hot tears, but he tamped it down. What kind of woman was Keri, that she was not only willing to accept what he'd told her, but eager to share these last few hours with him, so that he'd be able to pass on to the next life having known, for a few precious hours, paradise?

"You understand what I've said?" he asked, unable to disguise the emotion in his voice. So many feelings were churning inside of him now.

"Yes."

"And you still want to...are you sure?"

"How's this for sure?" Keri looped her arms around his neck and pulled, rising on tiptoes. "Take me again, Talen. Fuck me until there's no more time left."

Chapter Four

Pure, sweet joy tugged at his heart as he bent to kiss his sweet Keri. Her words still echoed in his ear, *Take me...fuck me until there's no time left.*

He'd finally found paradise, and how joyous a place it was. Warm. Glorious. Absolutely exquisite.

Her mouth softened beneath his, her lips parting to let him taste her. Their breath mixed, his and hers, their inhalations and exhalations working as one. Their tongues caressed and tasted. His mouth filled with her decadent flavor. The most delicious, intoxicating wine he had ever tasted.

More.

This time, he would force himself to go more slowly than the first time, to relish every stroke, kiss, sigh. After all, he would never again experience such magnificent joy. It would have to be enough to last an eternity.

He was determined to show Keri how grateful he was for her sacrifice. He would use his mouth, his hands, his tongue, lips, teeth, cock, every part of his body to show how much he appreciated her.

There was no way to tell her with words how much these moments meant to him. Only actions could communicate the depth of his emotions.

He flattened his hands on her lower back, pulling her tighter against him. Her clothed curves fit so perfectly against his harder angles and planes, one of the few differences between them. In so many other ways, ways that counted most, he felt like they were identical.

He slid his hands lower, over her round bottom and tipped his hips to grind his rigid erection against her.

Her lips still soft beneath his, she gave a quiet mewl, the sound tasting like sweet nectar as it slid over his tongue. "Talen," she whispered as she reached for his shoulders. "Ohmygod."

He smiled as she shuddered, fully appreciating the way her body responded to his every kiss, caress. "Mmmmm. How responsive you are."

"I can't help it when I'm with you."

"I'm glad." He let his hands wander up her back, fingertips tracing circles over her spine. In response, she arched slightly, pressing her abdomen even tighter against his hard rod, and dropped her head back.

Smiling to himself, he trailed tender kisses down the slender column of her neck, tarrying for a moment over the pulse beating strongly beneath the surface. It pounded quickly, seemingly in perfect timing with his thrumming heartbeat, and again he marveled at how perfectly their bodies worked together. How each touch and whimper ignited fires throughout his body. Her sighs whipped glittering sparks through his bloodstream, like burning embers exploding from a kicked log.

He ached to possess her hard and fast, to throw her to the ground, tear away her clothes and feast on her flesh. But he tamped down his feverish lust, vowing to take his time for both her sake and his.

She was touching him, holding him. Oh gods, the bliss.

For how long had he lived wrapped in a cocoon of icy air, an invisible bubble that he wouldn't let anyone break through? An eternity. Longer. He hadn't been held, kissed, or even enjoyed the simple pleasure of a hand in his for so many years. This was much more than a simple touch, the sensations so overwhelming, he almost became lost in them.

He pulled away, just letting his gaze wander over her, committing the sight of her beautiful face to his memory. That was the image he would keep with him as he passed from this world, those lovely eyes, perfect nose, lush mouth. He marveled at every detail of her face. Each freckle and eyelash, crease and curve. Arched brows. Smooth cheeks blushing a soft pink. Little chin, feminine and pointed.

"What's wrong?" she asked, her brows pulling down.

"Absolutely nothing." His gaze moved lower, halting at the neckline of her top. "Actually..."

Seeming to read his mind, she smiled, curled her fingers over the bottom edge of her shirt and pulled it up. Inch after inch of smooth porcelain skin was revealed.

He dropped to his knees, dragged his hands up the backs of her legs while simultaneously exploring every inch of that softly rounded surface with his tongue. His nose filled with her musk, and she quaked, bracing herself by planting her hands on his shoulders.

"You make my knees shake," she whispered.

"I feel them." He skimmed his hands back down, gently bracing her knees, helping to support them. Meanwhile, he continued to feast on her stomach, not able to let a single inch of skin go untasted.

With every thump of his heart, her weight bore down harder on his shoulders. Her shaking grew more violent. Her moans more urgent.

"Talen." She whimpered. "Help me."

Gently, he helped her to the floor, easing her onto her back. Their gazes met, and she smiled at him. Hair fanned around her face like a halo. So lovely. So perfect.

"Thank you," she said.

Unable to speak, his throat constricting tightly, he finished what she'd started, removing her shirt, her bra, her pants. Finally, she lay bare before him, her chest rising and falling with each swift breath. His gaze settled on her pink nipples, already hard. He knew they were delicious. He knew he had to have another taste.

He bent over and flicked his tongue over one turgid tip, savoring the sharp gasp his action elicited. In turn, his body hardened, a blaze of desire tearing through his bloodstream.

This woman was magic.

He drew that nipple into his mouth, enjoying the simple pleasure of tasting her skin, inhaling her scent. He suckled gently while using his fingers to tease the twin. As he sucked, he felt her curl her fingers into his hair, tugging slightly, the added sensation amplifying his carnal need.

Damn.

Stiff, burning with fever, and quickly losing control, he pulled on her nipple harder. He pinched her other one, rolling it between his finger and thumb, smiling when she moaned and pulled his hair, practically smashing his face into her soft flesh.

"Oh God, Talen. Just take me. Please."

"No." He unfurled her fingers from his hair and sat back. "You're going to get me. But not yet. I'm going to take it slowly, make you burn for me so bad, you're going to beg for relief."

"I already am." She lifted her hips, as if to illustrate.

"This is nothing." He dragged an index finger down the seam of her swollen nether lips, smoothing her sweet juice over her skin. Then he lifted his hand to his mouth and licked every drop away.

Her eyes widened. She shuddered. "Bastard."

"You'll thank me later."

"So cocky. You'd better live up to that promise."

"Haven't I already?" He pressed gently on her pelvis until she was lying flat again. Then, not waiting for her to respond, he pulled her knees apart and stroked her wet pussy. Soft, teasing touches. The air filled with the intoxicating scent of her arousal. "Have you ever had a lover take care with your needs, Keri? Has any man denied his own pleasure and focused on you?"

She squirmed, rocking her hips back and forth. "Maybe for a short time."

He pressed down on her thighs, stilling her motion. "Like ten minutes? Fifteen?" He bent his fingers, letting the tips dig slightly into her soft curves.

She arched her back, lifting her spine off the floor. "Yes, could be. I wasn't timing him or anything."

He smiled at the sight before him. Her ivory skin, so smooth and perfect. The heat in her eyes. "What about a half hour? An hour? Two?" He flattened his hands, dragging them up the sides of her thighs.

She tightened her legs, the muscles forming hard knots beneath the supple satin of her skin. "Never."

He moved his hands to the insides of her thighs and slowly eased them apart. "I will."

"Are you for real, Talen?" She shut her eyes, rocking her head from side to side. "Hours? You'd kill me if you did that."

He gazed down at the juncture of her thighs. Her folds unfurled, like petals of a blossom opening to the sun. He moistened his finger and touched the outer lips, licking his lips at the sight of those delicate tissues, glistening with her nectar. "No, no. You won't die. Just wait."

She reached for him. "That's just it, I don't want to."

He straddled her legs, caught her wrists in his hands, lifted them up over her head and pinned them to the floor, levering over her until the tip of his nose nearly touched hers. "Ah, but that's okay. I can make you wait, even if you don't want to."

She met his gaze, her eyes glittering with carnal need. "But that's just...mean."

"Perhaps. But, in another way, it's also most definitely kind." He felt the corners of his mouth lifting. The hairs on his nape bristled as a fevered chill swept up his spine. Hot. Cold. The sensations blended, one into the other. Goose bumps pricked the skin of his back and shoulders. His arms. "You'll come so hard, you'll feel it in your teeth." He bent lower, his mouth a fraction of an inch from hers. "The roots of your hair. The tips of your toes."

"Yessss."

He kissed her again, harder this time. His tongue plunged into the lush depth of her mouth, stroking hers, forcing it into submission. He tasted and took. Claimed. Possessed. And she relaxed beneath him, mewling softly into their joined mouths. Her wrists twisted in his grasp, and he loosened his grip, splaying his fingers as he slid them up toward her hands. They grasped hands, fingers curling, palms meeting.

He broke the kiss, but only to pepper her face and neck with kisses. His cock was hard as hewn rock. Balls tight. Blood hotter than molten lava. Still, he struggled to control the dark urges pounding through his body like the heavy beat of a drum.

Breaking away from her again, he sat back, tearing at his shirt. Off it came and then he disposed of his pants just as quickly.

He wouldn't take her yet. Couldn't. But he still ached to feel her touch him. Everywhere.

She lay on her back. Watching him. Glassy eyes full of fever but following his every move. Her kiss-swollen lips were parted into a natural pout. Unbelievably sexy.

Slowly, she rose up on one elbow. One of her hands skimmed down the lush curve of her stomach. It stopped at the juncture of her thighs, and a fierce jealousy blazed through his system.

"No." His voice was low, like an animal's warning growl.

Her brows lifted. "No, what? I'm not allowed to touch myself?"

"No, you're not." Nude, he went onto all fours and crawled over top of her, his legs straddling her hips, his hands her shoulders. "That's my job."

"I was getting impatient."

"It's been less than two minutes."

She sighed, those delicious lips of hers curling into a playful smile that made him think all kinds of wicked thoughts. "Two minutes too long."

He tsked as he forced her hands back up over her head. "You are impatient, aren't you?"

"I tried to warn you."

"Mmmmm." Releasing her hands, he trailed his

fingertips down her arms, over her shoulders and along the sides of her torso. He watched her face as he touched her, the smoldering fire in her eyes making him that much more desperate for her.

Down he continued, passing by her full breasts, the sensuous swell of her hips, to her knees. Once again, he pulled them apart.

This time, he was determined to savor her flesh, eat away every drop of her honey. Inhaling deeply, he bent over her, parting her labia with his fingertips. She was wet already, her folds glistening. Tempting.

He salivated. Spikes of erotic hunger pierced his insides. The scent of her musk filled his nostrils, honing those agonizing spikes.

He felt alive for the first time in eons. Fully human.

Just as he had her nipple, he flicked his tongue over her clit, tasting her juices. Sweet nectar. So delicious. He needed more. Shaking now, drowning in his need, he suckled her delicate tissues, pulling her flavor into his mouth, stabbing his tongue into her slit.

Beneath him, she rocked her hips slowly, forward and back, seeming to move to the thrumming beat pounding through his body. It was as if some primitive heartbeat was thumping through both of them.

He slipped a finger inside her, practically shivering at the way her slick canal clamped around it. He stroked her, licked, sucked until the heat radiating off her skin felt like a simmering wave, and her moans and whimpers turned to choked pleas for release. Then he stopped, slipped on a condom—this time finding the task much easier than the first. He rewarded himself by kissing his way back up her body, finally settling his hips between her spread thighs.

He wrapped his fingers around the base of his dick and dragged the swollen tip up and down along her slit but he didn't allow himself to take her. Not yet.

Damn, he just didn't want this to end.

He gazed down at her flushed face. Pink cheeks. Heavy lids fringed with long, sooty lashes. Lips pursed in a sex-kitten pout. That was a face he could stare at forever and never tire of the sight. So lovely. Impossibly beautiful.

He kissed her some more. He stroked her cheeks, her skin like warm rose petals. He nibbled her chin and kissed her eyelids, letting her fluttering lashes tickle his lips. He licked along her jaw and nipped her earlobe before burying his face in the crook of her neck and finally lunging his hips forward. His cock slid into her sheath to the hilt and a groan of pleasure rumbled in his chest.

Keeping his hips still, he nuzzled her neck, bit the swell of a shoulder. Underneath him, she arched her back, and his cock slipped deeper into her slick passage. So hot. Tight. Perfect.

God, how long it had been since he'd enjoyed a woman twice in one lifetime. Hell, it had been centuries since he'd had one at all.

He didn't want to think how long it would be until the next time he held a soft, warm body. Heard a woman's sigh. Smelled that intoxicating scent. Or enjoyed the pounding rush of his own heartbeat in his ears as he surrendered to the lust building between them.

Electricity charged the air. Tiny, invisible currents zapping between them, heating his skin and making it prickle and burn. He rocked his hips back, until the tip of his cock almost slipped from her pussy's grasp. Then, when he couldn't stand it anymore, he slammed them forward, driving his rod deep inside her again.

This time, their voices blended in a chorus of rapture.

Keri lifted her arms, her hands exploring his shoulders. When he thrust inside her a third time, she hooked her fingers, dragging her nails down his chest.

So many sensations. Such glorious bliss.

Too much. Heat. Wanting. Need.

He threw his head back and surrendered to his body's need, driving in and out of Keri's pussy. Hard and fast, he took her, until he was there, at the pinnacle. "No," he growled. He stopped.

The rough sound of his breathing, echoed by hers, filled his ears.

"You. Bastard." Her face twisted with fury, she pounded against his chest with her fists. "I was right there. Oh. My. God."

"I'm sorry, but I promised." He kissed her cheek. Her other cheek. Her nose. Chin. Forehead. "Besides, I can't stand the idea that it's almost over."

She sighed. The corners of her mouth twitched. She

lifted her legs, looping them around his waist, which made his cock glide deep inside her. She locked her ankles, trapping him there. The tip nudged at the opening to her womb. "We can do it again, silly. I'm not going anywhere."

He bit back a response, deciding it was much better to kiss away her anger.

She didn't put up a fight. Instead, she threw her arms around his neck and pulled him tightly against her. Chest to chest. Slick skin to slick skin. Nose to nose. "What is it about you? There's something so infuriating and yet so...fascinating."

"I'm just me." He kissed her again, silencing her before she asked a question he couldn't answer. And then, just in case she recovered too quickly from the punishment his tongue gave her, he began moving inside her again. Slow thrusts at first, gradually speeding up.

Their gazes locked and his soul rejoiced, feeding from the connection they shared. Thousands of years of ice accumulated around his heart like a frigid, hard shell melted. As if they were one, their bodies worked in perfect harmony, giving and taking pleasure. The heat scorching the air between them radiated so brilliantly the world around them seemed to ripple and sway until nothing existed but the two of them, Keri's beautiful body and his own. Intense sensations rolled over him like waves tumbling over the beach.

Such torment.

Such ecstasy.

Keri sighed and moaned, her hips rocking back and forth to meet his angry thrusts. She mapped every inch of his arms, chest and stomach with her hands while, eyes shut, she arched her spine and took the pleasure he gave her.

He fought his body's demand for release. Every second became a battle, and each battle made him feel more battered and overcome. This moment was like nothing he'd ever experienced before. Magical. Beyond words.

"Please," she whispered, once again clawing at him. Fingernails raked down his chest, leaving a tingling, burning wake of pleasure-pain behind. "I'm begging now. Like you said. Begging."

Her words were like a razor, slicing through his willpower.

Snap. Done.

Powerless to stop himself, he pounded into her hungry pussy, devoured her breasts with his mouth. She tangled her fingers in his hair again, alternately tugging him away and slamming him back down into her fragrant breasts over and over. Somehow, he slid a hand between their writhing bodies. He found her hard little clit and stroked it, slowly.

"Yesssss," she cried out. "Ohthankgod, yes!" Her body quaked. Her pussy tightened around his rod, like a warm, wet fist, milking him.

Tingles gathered in his gut. Exploded out like a detonated firework until his whole body zapped. Tension coiled, pulling him tight, tighter. Come burned at the base of his cock, ripped down its length and finally escaped his body. He heard himself growling.

Harder, faster, he plunged into her. His orgasm pulsed through his body, wave after wave. So fucking good. He didn't stop thrusting until the waves stopped. Until he was too exhausted to move. Until Keri sighed beneath him.

Her hands still moved, lightly tracing the lines carved between the muscles of his abdomen and chest. "That was...I don't know if there's a word to describe it."

He kissed her forehead. Eyelids. Cheeks, both of them. Chin. And finally, her mouth. The kiss was tender, filled with all the raw emotion he couldn't really wrap his head around. She kissed him back then blinked open her eyes.

Glittering eyes, full of emotion, just like his probably were.

He cupped her face. "Thank you."

"No, thank you. Sex has always been fun, but wow...that was just..."

A frigid chill swept up his spine. He pulled from her body, sat up and tugged off the spent condom.

"What's wrong?"

His hand smacked over the burning skin on the back of his neck, and he silently cursed the bastard who was right now stalking closer, the bastard who was determined to kill the woman beneath him.

Dammit. His time with her was over.

Not enough time. Not close to enough.

"He's back."

"Already?" She scrabbled to her feet. "Are you sure?" Eyes wide, she wrapped her arms around herself.

He scooped up a piece of her clothing and handed it to her. "Yes. He's back. This is it."

"No. Not so soon." Expression dark, she accepted the proffered garment and tugged it over her head. "Can't we...I don't know, run away? Hide? Stop him somehow?"

Run away. If only it were that simple.

Never had he hurt so badly at the thought of saying goodbye to another human being. It felt like his insides were being torn from his body. His heart pulverized.

He'd always believed his curse was cruel, but until this moment, he'd never fully appreciated how brutal.

If he could, if the gods who had cursed him would ever give him the chance, he would pay any price to be free. And it wasn't because of his pain that he made this wish, but the suffering he saw in Keri's eyes.

"I mean, I kinda knew you'd leave sooner or later. I can deal with that." She lifted her gaze to his. "But not yet. Please, not yet. Tell me there's some way to buy more time. Hours. A day, maybe. Just a little more."

Chapter Five

Keri knew she was being unreasonable—at least, if she believed what Talen had said about the curse. She didn't, of course. Who would? But what she did believe was that they had a short time, for whatever reason. And she respected him for being honest at least about that. He hadn't made a bunch of empty promises to try to get into her pants. Only a few sensational claims that he couldn't expect her to believe. Nobody was that gullible.

The fact was she'd been okay with the idea of a one-night fling. More than okay. Until now.

The sensation of him moving inside her was still there, between her legs. The friction. The heat. My God, the man was the most attentive, giving lover she'd ever been with. Sex with him was mind-blowing.

The first time they'd fucked had been something. The second time...she didn't know how to put it into words. Good thing she didn't need to.

But gah! She didn't need a boyfriend. She didn't want a boyfriend. Or even a steady lover. No commitments. No responsibilities. Nobody else to worry about. That was the way she lived. She just needed more time to say goodbye to him. That was all.

Surely, this curse thing was a farfetched story, a joke. Oddly, she'd sensed not a flicker of amusement or deception when he told her about it. Quite the opposite, he'd seemed to be telling the truth. Then again, she supposed it could be some kind of superstition, like how her palms itched before she received unexpected money. Or perhaps some kind of strange coincidence.

How strange a coincidence it was if people were attacked every time the back of his neck burned. Made her doubly grateful that nothing bad happened when her palms itched.

Curses don't really exist, she reminded herself.

And men didn't really live for hundreds of years.

Made her feel bad about the guy. It couldn't be easy, living that way, believing someone would die every time she got a tingle on her neck. Wow, she couldn't imagine...

Maybe she could show him that the curse wasn't real.

She shook her head.

Why should she try? This wasn't going anywhere, and he'd probably resent it anyway. People tended to get defensive when someone attacked their beliefs, however out-there they might be. That settled it, whatever his deal was, she didn't need to worry about it, since they'd be saying goodbye and he'd go on his miserable-not-really-cursed way and she'd continue living as she always had...

Geesh, I'm so freaking cold and selfish.

She glanced at him.

He was dressed. Peering out the window. Eyebrows furrowed. Arms crossed over his chest.

He looked like he had the weight of the world on his shoulders. And it suddenly became clear—it didn't matter whether the curse was real or not, to him it was, and he was obviously miserable.

"Is there anything I can do...to help?" She felt foolish for even saying the words.

One hand rubbing the back of his neck, he shook his head. "No." He turned to her. "You've done more for me than anyone has in centuries. I...I'd forgotten what it felt like to be touched. Held. Kissed."

Good God, if he had been telling the truth that would be awful. She liked to keep people at arm's length, and she had her own reasons for doing so. But she still had sex when she wanted. Evidently, it had been a long time for Talen. Months or years even.

Centuries?

Just imagining living for hundreds of years but not having someone to talk to, vent to or laugh with made her feel cold and empty.

"You really believe you've lived hundreds of years?" she asked, expecting one answer while wishing she'd hear another.

Standing by the window, he shrugged. "Sure."

The response she'd expected. "What was it like back then? The world?"

"In some ways, just like it is now. Mankind is still the

same. Always searching for whatever might make him happy next, buy him a few moments of contentment. The clothes he wears and the things he clings to are just different."

"You're jaded."

"I've seen too much not to be."

"What about the good? You must have seen some good things too."

He rubbed his neck again.

"Is our time up?"

He turned back toward the window. "No, but it will be soon."

"How soon?"

"Minutes."

Her heart lurched, and she leaned toward him, suddenly eager to feel his strong arms wrapped around her again. "We managed to escape him once before. Can we do it a second time?"

He stared at her for a long, tense moment, his expression completely unreadable.

"Maybe we could snag a few more hours?" she asked when he didn't say anything. She felt her face warming. "I mean, you want more time, don't you?"

He gathered her into a tight embrace and she gladly sank into it, soaking up his heat. Safe. Protected. Warm. She'd never felt better. "I do. I really do."

"So do I."

He cupped her chin, brushed his mouth over hers.

"I don't expect forever," she told him. "You don't have to make up stories to let me off easy, if that's what you're doing."

"I wish this all was a lie. It's not." He gazed at her, some kind of emotion brewing in his eyes.

She didn't speak, just savored the moment, the way he looked at her, the energy charging through the air, the sensation of his strong arms wrapped protectively around her like a cocoon.

"Oh, hell. Let's go." As if a switch had been thrown, hurling him into frenzied action, he headed toward the door.

"Hang on! Let me get my stuff, at least." While he paced the floor, looking anxious, she scurried about, gathering the things she'd brought from her apartment. A few minutes later, Talen led her out of the building, gaze snapping back and forth, all around them. Once they were in the parking lot, he hesitated.

"Did you forget where you're parked?" she asked.

"I don't own a car."

"Mine's over there in my reserved spot—"

"No, we'll walk." He closed his hand around hers and tugged her down the street. To keep pace, she had to fall into a jog-slash-race walk. It left her short-winded, so she didn't talk. Neither did he, for quite a while.

They hurried down tree-lined streets, past stores and restaurants, homes and parks. Finally, about two miles from the building, he slowed enough so she could walk instead of run.

"Thank you," she said between huffs. She glanced over her shoulder. "Do you think we're being followed?"

"The sensation's cooling."

"You're like a walking, talking bad-guy Lojack, aren't you? How handy," she quipped.

"I've never tried to avoid them before. Always believed the worst would happen if I did."

"What made you do it this time?"

He smiled down at her. "Do you really need to ask?"

"Is it just the sex?"

"No, actually, it's not."

Silence. A few fat raindrops smacked her on the head. A wind gust caught her hair, sending it whipping across her eyes.

"It isn't for me either," she admitted.

More silence. More raindrops.

She shoved her hair back, away from her face. It was quickly becoming a soggy, matted mess. And her clothes were getting wet too. She tugged at her cotton shirt to keep it from clinging to her skin and giving passersby a look at her goods. "Where are we headed? Do you have any idea?"

He shoved his fingers through his damp hair. The ends were curling. His skin was glistening. His damp clothes starting to adhere themselves to his glorious body. He looked uber sexy. "No. I'm not familiar with the area. Do you have any ideas?"

She pointed east. "There's a hotel down there. But we

don't have any money."

"That's okay. I'll take care of it. How far down?" A droplet of rainwater fell from a curl hanging over the center of his forehead. It landed on his nose then dribbled down to the tip where he wiped it away. "I hope it's close. You're getting drenched."

"I'm okay. It feels kind of good." She squinted, futilely trying to mentally tick off how many traffic lights there were between their current position and the intersection in front of the hotel. She just couldn't think straight, not with a very wet and tempting Talen standing next to her. "I'm guessing it's another two miles or so. Funny, but when you're driving, you don't pay attention to how many miles away something is. Distances just don't mean the same thing."

"So true," he agreed, palming her cheek.

Their gazes locked and all she could think about was how wonderful he tasted and what an amazing kisser he was. Just when she thought he might bend down and give her another taste of that luscious mouth of his, he dropped his hand and started to walk again. "Try traveling five hundred miles by foot."

"You've walked five hundred miles?" she asked, admiring his shoulders and arms. The man had to spend more than his share of time in the gym with a physique like that.

"Yes."

Growing annoyed with her hair, she gathered it at her nape in a fist. "I can't even wrap my head around that notion. It's like what? The distance from New York to...I can't even guess. How long did it take?" She stopped walking, propping herself up with a tree trunk. Her tennis shoe had come untied. "Hang on a second."

He dropped to a knee, and once again, she found herself looking into the darkest eyes she'd ever seen. So many shadows. "Over a month," he said.

"Huh?"

"That's how long it took to walk five hundred miles."

"Oh!" She shook her head, which seemed to be filled with molten gelatin instead of grey matter. "Um, wow." She watched as Talen tied her shoe. His fingers worked deftly. Nicely shaped. They were long and tapered, with neatly trimmed nails. And they did some wonderful things to her body sometimes.

A little gush of warmth rushed through her system.

He flashed a smile that was so stunning it nearly knocked her to her knees, then pushed to stand. That adorable curl, dripping wet and hanging over the center of his forehead, was screaming for her to play with it. "Ready?" he asked.

"Yeah." Somewhat dizzy, she shuffled along beside him, shaking her head. He was something special. Dangerous. Extremely so. Attentive. Striking. Beautiful. She tried to keep their meaningless conversation going, fearing what might come out of her mouth if the topic turned to more serious matters. "A year-long walk. I'd die before I arrived at my destination."

"One year's nothing. Moses and the Hebrews

wandered the desert for forty years."

"Did they truly? I hate to admit I don't remember my Bible stories very well."

He smiled, nodding. "They sure did."

Returning his grin, she stopped walking long enough to throw her weight to one hip. Mocking him, she asked, "And you remember this because...were you with them?" As they stood there, rain plunking on their heads, their clothes sticking to their bodies, she noticing his gaze had wandered south a smidge, and having some inkling why, she pulled on the sodden material of her shirt again. She glanced down and sent up a silent thanks that she was wearing black. At least it wasn't see-through.

He leaned forward, grasping her hands and pulling them behind her back. He stared down into her eyes for a handful of racing heartbeats. The tip of his tongue swept across his lower lip. Her body tingled as expectation sent warm waves rushing up and down her spine. He jerked on her hands, pulling her flush against him. Soft feminine curves against hard masculine angles. They fit together so perfectly.

He tipped his head. Lower, lower still.

Oh yes. Kiss me! She closed her eyes.

"I was born about three hundred years after Moses led the Hebrews out of Egypt."

"Huh?" No kiss? Tease.

"I just remember the story." He released her, and she threw her hands out to steady herself. Her knees were wobbly, her head spinny. What this man did to her!

"Three hundred years after Moses," she said, not truly comprehending what she was saying. Her mind was occupied by other thoughts. Ones that involved his mouth and hands and a few bits of her anatomy. "That was when?"

"About 900 BCE." He took her hand, gently tugging her along as he began walking again.

"Nine hundred years *before* Christ? Um, that was a long time ago."

"Yes, it was."

She studied his profile as they walked. He was amazing from every angle, in every light, wet, dry, standing, sitting. Even when he was talking nonsense, about living thousands of years. "I guess you have seen a lot."

His expression darkened. "More than any man should."

"More than I think I'd want to." Silence. She tried to catch her breath, sort through her racing thoughts. "I'm sorry about the curse."

The energy between them changed instantly. "It's done. It just is."

He honest-to-God believed there was a curse. Whether he truly believed he was almost three thousand years old was yet to be determined. "How do you deal?"

"I don't. I exist. That's all. And I exist because I can't do anything else."

If curses were real, and people could live for

thousands of years, just existing would take a ton of strength. Willpower. More than she had. Such despair, isolation, loneliness. Suffering. Desperation. "I think I'd kill myself," she muttered.

"I'd still come back to life."

Shit, he heard me. She smacked her hands over her mouth. "That was a stupid thing to say. I'm so sorry."

"It's okay." He didn't look upset as he gently pulled her hands from her face. "You're being real. I think anyone cursed like me would at least think about killing himself."

She wanted to ask him if he had thought about suicide, but she couldn't say the words. It wasn't right, talking like this. The curse might be all in his head but she knew the suffering and loneliness she saw in his eyes was one hundred percent real.

Such a good man, too. He deserved so much more in life.

If only there was some way to help him break free from his belief. Maybe then he could have the happiness he so desperately wanted.

"This curse seems unbelievably harsh. Nobody could do something so bad that they deserve to suffer like that."

"The gods disagree."

How could she convince him that his curse wasn't a punishment delivered by a divine being, but more likely a series of coincidences? She dropped the subject, hoping inspiration would strike later.

She pointed at the three-story beige building ahead. "Our home-away-from-home. I'm hungry. It's gotta be close to noon by now, and we haven't eaten yet. Should we grab something to eat first? We can take it up to our room. I'd like to get out of these wet clothes right away." She patted the bag she wore slung over her shoulder. "I hope this thing's waterproof."

"Sure. We can do that."

They stopped at the closest restaurant, a cozy Mexican place with a dark, romantic interior and the mouthwatering smell of grilled meat. Every table was packed, waiting diners gathered in the lobby.

They got lucky, finding two seats at the bar, and the bartender, a short brunette woman, handed them menus. "Hi there. Looks like you two got caught in a downpour."

"We sure did," Talen responded before turning to Keri. "Order whatever you want. I've got it covered."

"Okay. Thanks." It was strange, that this place had been there all this time, so close to home, and yet she'd never bothered to check it out before. "Mmmm. I'm starving and something smells really good. How about one of each?" Everything on the menu looked scrumptious. She scooped up a handful of tortilla chips from the basket the bartender set before them and weighed her options.

Beside her, Talen chuckled. "If you ate one of each, I'd be impressed."

She grinned. "I might not be able to put away this much food, but I can do some serious damage at an all-you-can-eat buffet. I like food."

"Yet another reason why I find you adorable." He leaned over and kissed her, and she couldn't help—for the briefest moment—feeling like she was simply on a date with a gorgeous guy.

Then reality slapped her in the face when Talen grimaced and rubbed the back of his neck.

"Do we need to leave?" she whispered. Even though she didn't believe Talen was cursed, his burning neck had been followed by an attack. She was willing to accept that he had some kind of sensitivity or sixth sense to danger that manifested itself in a physical way. No doubt, his work had something to do with it.

"Huh?" He gave her a bewildered look.

"Your neck."

"Oh." He dropped his hand and donned a sheepish grin. "It's a nervous habit, I guess. Nobody's ever pointed it out to me." He motioned to the menu in his hand. "Have you been here before?"

Relieved, she drew in a long, deep breath. "Nope."

"What're you getting, now that you've decided you're not taking everything?"

"Not sure yet." She grinned, loving this moment—apart from that handful of tense seconds. The glitter in Talen's eyes, the energy zapping between them, sensual heat coiling through her body once again. She'd never shared such an intense relationship with anyone before, at least not right out of the gate. Physically, mentally, emotionally, it felt right. She wondered if it was simply because she knew it wouldn't last forever.

The bartender set a couple of glasses of water before them, asking, "Are you ready to order yet? Or do you need a few more minutes?"

"Just a few more. Sorry," Keri responded.

The bartender smiled, grabbing a glass off the counter and dumping some ice into it. "Not a problem. Just holler when you're ready."

"Will do." Keri stared at the menu. "Guess we'd better get down to business."

Another chuckle. "There are so many comebacks I could give to that one."

"Hah. You are such a man."

"And I won't apologize for it either." He set down his menu. "I'm ready."

Keri did the same. "I guess I am too."

Talen flagged down the bartender—who was clearly the queen of multitasking—and they placed their orders. Talen paid the bill with cash. For a few minutes afterward, they sat in comfortable silence, watching the bartender dispense alcohol to chattering customers and harried-looking waitresses balancing round trays on their hands.

Growing weary, just from watching her, Keri decided it was more fun studying the man sitting next to her. He was looking straight ahead, a water glass in his fist, an intense expression on his face.

That was some face. Handsome, not pretty. Striking eyes. A straight nose that was neither too big nor too small. Lips that were absolutely scrumptious, slightly fuller than the average guy and yet still masculine. And that square jaw, now peppered with dark stubble that made him look a bit wild and naughty.

Stunning.

He finally seemed to sense she'd been staring at him. He smiled as he turned to look at her, twisting on the swivel seat so his entire body was facing her way. He pushed on the back of her stool, making it turn too, toward him. "You've gotten quiet."

"Yeah. I guess I have."

He parted his bent knees placing them on either side of hers and took her hand in his. "You're going to be okay. I won't let anything happen to you."

Ironically, she didn't know him but she believed what he said. Not only was she convinced he wouldn't let anything or anyone physically harm her, but she sensed if he had the chance, he would protect her in all ways. Even emotionally.

He was extremely attentive. Maybe that was why she felt so differently about him, compared to the other men she'd dated. When he was with her, he was *with* her. She had a feeling a gorgeous supermodel could walk into the room and he wouldn't notice. It was wonderful, feeling that important to another human being for once. Beyond wonderful, actually.

Nodding, she murmured. "Thanks. I mean, you saved my life. I owe you. Big time. Nobody's done much of anything for me in a long time."

"That's just wrong." He lifted one of her hands to his mouth and kissed her palm. "People should do amazing things for you every day."

Embarrassed, but also giddy, she snatched her hand away. "Stop it. I'm nobody special, just a regular girl."

"No, you're wrong. There's nothing regular about you." He cupped her cheek, his thumb tracing her lower lip. "Not your mouth. Or your eyes. Or your..." His gaze traveled lower.

"Breasts?" she whispered, adjusting her shirt again.

"No, heart." He chuckled. "I may be a man, but I think about more than sex."

Her insides melted a little.

After a moment, he added, "I can't believe I just said that. And by the way, you don't owe me anything."

"But we agreed I would pay your regular rate. What do you normally charge clients for your body-guarding services?"

"Nothing."

"You're all set," the bartender said, just as Keri was about to come up with some clever response to Talen's lie. The woman set a large paper bag on the bar. "Is there anything else I can get you two?"

"No, I guess not," Keri answered, gazing at Talen.

He shrugged and curled his fingers around the bag's handles. "Thank you." Standing, he offered his free hand to Keri. "Let me help you."

She accepted his offer, grinning like a total dork as

her fingers wove between his. "Such a gentleman." That smile didn't fade a bit as they walked through the crowded restaurant bar and lobby. Even outside, he didn't release her hand, and she was suddenly very appreciative of the simple pleasure of holding hands while walking down the street, the air scented with grass and flowers as a cool drizzle fell from swollen clouds overhead. As they turned the corner, stepping into the hotel's parking lot, he tightened his fingers and brushed his thumb over the back of her hand, and a buzzing zap sizzled through her body.

He held the door for her guiding her toward a couch in the lobby. "Would you like to wait here while I register?"

"Sure."

He set the bag of food next to her. "Be back in a minute."

She watched him walk away, once more marveling at what an amazing man he was, despite his one (slightly significant) quirk. She counted at least a dozen great qualities about him before he returned. He scooped up the bag of food, slung her overnight bag over his shoulder and they headed up to their new temporary home. The delicious scents of cheese and spiced meat accompanied them into the elevator, down the hall and into their room.

Two queen beds? She gave Talen a questioning glance when she stepped inside, and he smiled, revealing shallow dimples on either side of his mouth.

Placing the bag on top of a dresser, he shrugged. "I

didn't want to make any assumptions."

"You truly are one of a kind, you know that, don't you?" She headed into the bathroom to change. The clothes in her bag were dry—thank God. After dressing, she tidied up her hair and makeup and headed back into the room.

Talen had not only changed into dry clothes, but he also had their food all set up and was lounging on one of the beds, his back resting against the headboard, his foam container balanced on his lap, the television remote in his hand, and some sporting event on the television. He'd made himself right at home.

He patted the mattress. "Have a seat."

She kicked off her shoes and climbed up onto the bed, settling beside him. "Now this is the life."

He tucked a couple of pillows behind her back. Such a sweetheart. Then, once he seemed content that she was comfy, he handed her a foam container, fork and napkin. "We don't have anything to drink, but I saw a vending machine out by the elevators. Do you want something?"

"Sure. I'll take a diet cola, whatever brand they have." She watched him as he headed for the door. "Before you go...how's your neck?"

Reacting to her question, he slapped his hand over his nape. "Not even a tingle. Looks like we lost him. At least for a while."

"Hey, maybe we'll get lucky and it'll take him a few days to find us again. What do you think?"

"I don't know. I've never tried to outrun death before.

We're both treading new ground here."

"Well I've gotta admit, if I have to hide from a would-be murderer, I'm glad I'm with you." She shifted nervously, her heart thumping hard against her breastbone. "I mean, you make me feel safe."

His smile was genuine and warm and made her heart thump even harder. "I'm glad I'm with you too." He fisted the doorknob. "Be right back."

"Okay." The minute he left the room, she snatched up the remote and changed the channel. Sports were so not her thing. He was just going to have to live with it. Nice as he was, there were some things she couldn't let go.

She did, however, wait until he returned before starting to eat. And she did give him a beaming welcome-back smile when he handed her a can of diet cola. "Thank you."

"You're very welcome." He sat on the bed, close enough so his elbow brushed against her arm.

Finally, she flipped open the container and plucked a nacho chip from the cheese-coated mountain piled in the center. "Has anyone ever told you you're very polite?"

Chewing, he shrugged. "No. But I don't spend enough time with anyone for them to know."

After delivering more chips to her mouth, she shook her head, turning to look at him. "I know I said earlier that we are kind of the same—that neither one of us has anyone close to us. That we are somewhat isolated, but I can't imagine my life is anything like yours."

"Why is that? Why are you alone?"

"Because that's the way I like it." She dipped a chip into some cheese then popped it into her mouth.

"You intentionally cut yourself off from people?"

She chewed and swallowed before responding. "Sure. Maybe you don't realize this, but most people are assholes. Out for themselves. Manipulative. Lying. Male, female, doesn't matter. True and honest friendship is almost impossible to find—"

"And love?" he interrupted.

She chuckled. "Love. I know it's hard for you to believe. Maybe I'm being a bitch for saying this, but honestly, I wonder if you're better off being cursed."

He stiffened beside her, and she instantly regretted her words. Real or not, a curse was nothing to joke about.

"I'm sorry."

Eyes dark, expression a little distant, he nodded. "It's not your fault. Not being a whiner, but nobody can imagine what it's like walking in my shoes."

"No, you're right. But would you hate me if I said I kind of wish we could trade places?"

"No, I don't hate you. I'm sad for you, though. If you think hell is better than what you have now..."

"I did say 'kind of wish'. The dying part has to be beyond awful."

There was an awkward stretch of silence while they both ate. Finally, Talen broke it. "Tell me about you, about your work, your friends."

A change of topic. Probably a good thing.

As she nibbled on her nachos, she gave him the basics, about her job, which she loved, her love of naughty romance novels featuring fierce alpha men, her eBay addiction and favorite television shows. As she talked, the tension in the air eased. Their moods lifted. She intentionally avoided mentioning her friend issues, worrying things would get uncomfortable again. Instead, she kept things light and fun. She flirted a little, teasing him, meeting his gaze and then jerking her eyes away. Slanting a coy smile at him every once in a while. Scooting closer and offering to share some of her chips. Wiping away a drop of cheese that had dripped onto his chin.

She could feel the energy in the room changing. Tension building. But this time, it wasn't because she was saying stupid things and making him feel bad. It was one hundred percent lust charging the air.

Talen set his container aside then gently tugged hers out of her hand. "You still haven't answered my question." Twisting, he swung a leg over hers, straddling both. He planted his hands on the headboard, on either side of her head, basically caging her in.

Trapped. Literally and figuratively.

Had someone cranked on the heat?

"Which question was that?" she asked, grinding her spine into the headboard.

"The one about love."

"No, I answered."

He shook his head. "Nope."

Bastard.

"Love is...love is dangerous. But I do want to find someone to love. Someday."

"Dangerous? Why?"

"Because loving involves trusting. Commitment. Opening yourself up to heartbreak. Like I said, dangerous."

"I see." He leaned closer, brushed his mouth over hers. It wasn't really a kiss. More of a soft, teasing touch.

She shivered. Closed her eyes, fully expecting him to kiss her again. Harder.

He kissed her jaw. "Does that mean you don't spend time with men? You don't have lovers?"

"Oh no. Not at all. I've had my share. They're just never right. Wrong guy. Right time. Right guy. Wrong time. Wrong guy at the wrong time." She looped her arms around his neck, tipping her head to the side as he nibbled down her neck. "Do we really need to talk about this right now?"

"Yes. No. Maybe." He gave her butterfly kisses back up her neck then nipped her earlobe.

That was it, she was seriously melting again. "Have I told you how crazy that makes me?"

"What? This?" He did it again.

She shivered, and her skin puckered with goose bumps. "Yes, that." Tingles zapped under her skin, warming it.

"Then you wouldn't complain if I did it once more."

"Hell no." Her neck tightened. Expectation charged through her system. And yet, there was no nip. No nibble. No love bite.

Instead, he leaned back. "Tell me about your last lover."

Was he joking? She opened her eyes, checking his expression. Dead serious. "*Now?*"

"Sure."

"We're about to... Why do you want to know about that? What's it matter to you?"

"It just does. We won't get a lot of time together. I want to know everything about you."

"If we won't get a lot of time together, wouldn't it be better to spend what precious time we have doing other things, rather than talking?"

He frowned.

"I'm not trying to be mean or insensitive."

"Honest-to-God intimacy is precious to me." Looking annoyed, he shoved his fingers through his hair. "I sound like a girl, don't I?"

"No, of course not."

"I realize it's kind of illogical, what I'm asking. But I've waited so long, and been so lonely. I crave something. A feeling. No, it's not a feeling at all. It's an experience. I want you to be mine until our time is up. I want to know your secrets. Every single one."

What a terrifying thing to hear, and yet at the same time it was wonderful. Here was a man who could never be hers—at least if what he said was true. And yet, if he was truly cursed and unable to get close to anyone, was there a safer person on the planet to tell all her darkest secrets?

"You've been avoiding this, haven't you?" He tugged at a loose thread on the bottom of her tank top.

"What?"

He jerked his hand and the string snapped. He smoothed the bunched hem against her stomach. "It's not that you've met the wrong men or met them at the wrong time. You're not opening yourself up to the right ones."

She felt herself stiffening. *I didn't come to you for therapy.* She clamped her lips shut before a sarcastic comeback slipped past them.

Once again, he leaned forward, this time pressing his entire upper body against hers. "I'm not asking. I don't think you want me to. I'm telling you, you are mine until our time is up. Your body. Your mind. Your heart."

Confused, and needing some air, she shoved at his chest, but he caught her wrists and slammed them back against the headboard, holding her hostage. Then he kissed her hard, his mouth possessing her with all the fire she'd heard in his words.

Panic raced through her body, sending chills up her spine. And lust coursed through her veins, pumping heat out from her center.

Hot and cold.

Angry. Confused.

Resisting.

Can't surrender. Won't.

Chapter Six

How had things suddenly gone so wrong? One minute, they had been sharing a nice moment. Flirting. Teasing. Driving each other crazy in a good way. And the next, Talen had changed, acting possessive, domineering. Dammit, she didn't need this.

And she didn't want to think about why she was getting so fricking turned on.

"Stop!" Twisting away, she broke the kiss to drag in a deep breath. And while Talen sucked and bit her neck, she clamped her eyes closed and shoved his chest as hard as she could.

He didn't stop. Sadly, her push didn't budge him either. Instead, he clapped a hand over her breast, squeezing the soft flesh, kneading it. "Have you ever had a man treat you like this? A little rough. Dominating."

"Hell no. I don't like it." As she writhed beneath him, her heart whapping against her ribcage and her blood simmering, her words were beginning to look like lies. But she wasn't about to tell him the truth. It would encourage him to continue. She pushed at him again. "What the hell just happened?"

"I touched your breast." He squeezed, no doubt to illustrate.

Annoyed but also bordering on overcome by lust, she growled. Literally. "No, before that."

"I bit your neck." Again, he repeated the action.

"Before that." Flinching, and trying to convince her body that it didn't need to produce goose bumps and lustful quivers, she pushed him a third time. "I mean, why'd you change from polite but protective bodyguard to domineering caveman?"

"When I realized I could do something more for you than simply take a fucking bullet or knife in the gut."

What?

He jerked away, rolling off the bed and charged to the bathroom, shutting the door. Finally, she could catch her breath and sort through the horde of emotions blazing through her system. Shaky still, she scooped up her nachos, clicked through the channels and tried to shut off her brain for a few minutes.

Things were getting too fucking intense. Gauging from the questions he'd asked, he knew she wasn't looking for intense. And if what he said was true, that he was going to die at any moment, what was the point in all this?

Nobody acted this way, staking a claim to a woman they'd never see again. Not if they were going to die tomorrow. Hell, plenty of men avoided committing to a woman under normal circumstances.

Men liked to fuck. And fucking was what they'd done up until now. Hot sex. No strings. Fucking.

A thought struck her hard, like a concrete block slamming into her head. She saw stars.

What kind of asshole would...?

No, that couldn't be true...!

Unless he was an absolute psycho...

Since he'd told her about his supposed curse and extraordinary lifespan, she'd suspected him of telling some tall tales to impress her. But for whatever reason, she hadn't considered the worst before now.

Could he have orchestrated the break-in and the attack, just to get her to spend some time with him?

She jumped off the bed, suddenly too jittery to sit. She headed back toward the bathroom door. Glared at it for a moment. Then, she turned and headed in the opposite direction, toward the room's exit.

Proof. Did she have any?

She stared at the small gym bag he'd brought from his apartment. Did she dare sneak a peek?

The break-in would be easy enough to fake. If he was truly a bodyguard, he probably knew how to pick a lock. He could have lied about the whole thing. Who knew, maybe the cufflink he'd claimed to find in her apartment had been there all along, and she simply hadn't found it yet.

Completely believable scenario. But again, she had no proof. There was a thump in the bathroom, the squeak of faucets turning. Her gaze snapped to the door.

Faking a burglary put him in the Most Definitely

Sneaky But Not Necessarily Dangerous category. Manipulative, yes. Underhanded, sure.

The police. He'd promised to call, but had he? He hadn't mentioned it. She hadn't been asked to write up a statement. Hadn't had so much as a phone conversation with a police officer.

Very suspicious. Perhaps he hadn't called because he didn't want to face the consequences.

What about the attack? That was a totally different thing. If Talen knew the guy with the knife, had paid him to hang around for a few days and stalk her, that was beyond unforgivable. It was sick. Demented. Desperate.

Her gaze locked on the closed door, she inched toward the bag.

Why would he do such a thing? First, she was hardly the kind of woman men went to such extreme measures to get. Second, they'd barely spoken since he'd moved in. But they had flirted a bit. Still, it wasn't like she'd rebuffed him, making him think he had to stoop to such tricks. If anything, he should have recognized the I'm-interested vibe she'd been sending.

Again, things weren't adding up.

The bathroom doorknob rattled.

Shitshitshit. Halfway between the bag and the exit, she froze in place.

At this point, she really, really wanted to walk out that door. But whether he was a liar or telling the truth, she had to expect that there was either a pretend stalker-slash-fake-killer or a real stalker-slash-genuine-killer waiting for her. Out there. Somewhere.

Wow. She'd been an idiot to trust him the way she had. But she blamed her lack of using proper judgment on his chest. And his stomach. And his face. Shoulders. Arms. If he hadn't been in her kitchen, wearing a towel, she wouldn't have seen any of those body parts and chances were she wouldn't have been so willing to trust him without knowing anything about him.

A curse. What a joke.

A man who'd lived hundreds of years. How could she be so stupid?

Dumb. Gullible. Blind. It was her lust that had blinded her.

Not any longer. She hurried over to the bag and unzipped the front pocket, pulling it open. Until she was absolutely clear what this man was up to, she would have to keep him at a distance. Physically. Emotionally. Mentally. She shoved her hand inside, grabbed a fist full of contents.

She'd have to be strong. She'd have to...

The doorknob rattled again, and she yanked her hand out and sprinted toward the opposite side of the room.

The bathroom door swung open and a cloud of steam billowed into the room, rolling like a fog drifting up a beach on a breeze. The scent of lavender teased her nose as he sauntered out, once again sporting his favorite garment—a towel. His hair was a riot of spiky, wet waves. Little droplets of water glistened over his back, chest, arms and shoulders.

Strong. She had to stay strong. At this point, it was only a theory, but...this beautiful man could be some kind of deranged stalker, orchestrating bizarre situations to get women into his clutches. He might be devious. A fiend. A killer, even.

Wow, fiend or not, he had the most perfect body she'd ever laid eyes on.

Cover up those abs. Please! And the chest. And the shoulders too.

He didn't speak as he strolled into the room. Instead, he just stared at her, his expression totally unreadable.

She decided it was a good time to watch television and tried to tear her gaze free from his. It didn't work.

God, she was so effing weak.

Remember your worries! This guy could be the worst kind of trouble. Good-looking men were always bad news. And didn't it make sense then, that this amazing-looking one would be that much worse?

She didn't know what to do now. Should she confront him, and give him the chance to confess? Or should she just play along, until she could find some way to safely escape?

Argh, she wasn't thinking straight. He could just as easily be a real bodyguard trying to protect her from danger. She was afraid. Scared to trust him. Petrified about what she did know about all this and even more terrified about what she didn't.

Dammit, if her best friend were only in town. Lori had left a couple nights ago to attend a romance book convention in Florida. While Lori was stomping around in fairy costumes, snapping pictures of her favorite authors and filling her suitcase with free books, there was a major crisis going on here.

Keri glanced at her purse, thinking it might be a good time to take a shower. The sound might muffle her voice...she hoped. Not that her friend could do anything to help her, down in the land of the alligators and Mickey Mouse, but she needed someone to talk to, a level head to help her decide what to do next.

Heading for her purse, she said, "I think I'll get cleaned up too. It's been a long day and I feel dirty."

"It's all yours." He made a sweeping gesture toward the bathroom then watched her like a predator tracking its prey as she rushed by. "I need to make a call to the police while you're getting cleaned up."

Hmmm, so he hadn't called the police yet. What made him think to do it now?

"Good idea." Inside, she locked the door, cranked on the shower and frantically dug into her purse for her phone. She checked the time—it was the middle of the afternoon. Lori had told her she would keep her cell phone on this year. Last year she'd shut it off right after she boarded the plane and didn't turn it back on until she stepped foot back in Detroit's Metro airport. She punched in her friend's cell number and crossed her fingers.

One ring.

Two.

Three.

Four.

Not looking good.

Then, she heard that telltale break.

Her call was going to voicemail. Damn.

She cupped her hand around the phone and turned toward the back wall, hoping her voice would be muffled. "Hey. You leave, and all hell breaks loose. I need you to call me back. Like now. Pleasepleaseplease get this message." She snapped the phone shut, went into her overnight bag, found the charger and plugged it in.

Not knowing what else to do, and liking the idea of killing a little time, she went ahead and took a shower. She washed. Washed again. Shaved everywhere. Just stood there, letting the hot water beat on her back. Finally, fearing she'd be a puckered prune for days, she cut off the water and got out.

She stared at the phone as she dressed.

It didn't ring.

Still on edge, she studied the door for a while. Finally, she opened it.

Quietly crept into the room.

And released a huge sigh.

Talen was lying on his back, one arm thrown up over his head, the other resting on his torso. The television remote lay beside his hand. His eyes were closed. His breathing slow, deep and steady.

Sleeping.

This was it—the perfect opportunity. She could run

away. Go to the police. Call the police. Do something besides sit there and wait for someone else to give her answers.

The police station. It was only a few miles. A short stroll.

She headed back to the bathroom, quickly gathered her things. Arms loaded, she tiptoed across the room, to the door, watching Talen as she hurried past him.

She stopped at the door, gently twisted the knob. Pulled it open. But when it came time to walk out, she couldn't make herself do it. Not with the memory of that attack in her apartment so fresh in her mind.

A million what-ifs flew through her head. What if the killer was out there, waiting for her? What if Talen wasn't the fiend she suspected? What if the police didn't help her? Did she have any proof that she'd been attacked? What if she didn't make it to the police?

Her gaze swept the room again, and she noticed a white business card sitting on the nightstand. She set down her things and plucked up the card.

It belonged to a police officer.

Talen had called the police. When? While she was sleeping at Talen's apartment? Or here at the hotel, while she was in the shower?

This only raised more questions. The policeman hadn't asked to talk to her. Why not? Had he blown off the complaint? Or perhaps he would be returning later, after checking out some things?

Nonono. If Talen had called the police, the officer

would have insisted on talking to her. He would have taken a statement. Talen had put the card there to make her think he'd called.

Still, she had no proof of anything. Only lots of suspicions.

Her determination waned, and what had seemed such a brilliant plan suddenly seemed like a really dumb idea. It was one thing to wonder if Talen had something to do with the attack. A wise person considered all possibilities when facing a life-or-death situation. But it was foolish to take stupid risks.

She was no fool.

But she was thoroughly exhausted from all the stress. And even though the clock said it was only a little after three in the afternoon, her body told her it was much, much later.

Would it be wise to get some rest now?

Silently, she cut off the lights, crept over to the other bed, slipped beneath the covers and closed her eyes, hoping she'd be able to fall asleep. Even the slightest stress kept her awake at night. This situation was beyond *slightly* stressful.

She closed her eyes and tried to imagine something pleasant. Her body grew heavy. She felt herself drifting, drifting...

Talen heard Keri's breathing slow down and deepen. The moment he was certain she was asleep, he rolled over to face her. Although their room wasn't on the ground level, they'd kept the room-darkening curtains drawn. She'd shut off all the room's lights, but the television still offered muted illumination. It was enough to provide him with a dazzling view.

In sleep, her face took on an angelic, sweet expression, as he'd expected it would the first time he'd seen her. Her features were relaxed, lips slightly parted, the corners curled up a little. A Mona Lisa smile.

He wondered what she was dreaming about.

Not at all tired, he piled his pillows on top of each other to prop himself up a little. She was fascinating, both asleep and awake. Gods help him, he couldn't get enough of her.

Thoughts of their earlier discussion raced through his mind. What she'd said was true—he had no right asking the questions he had. She wasn't his. He had no claim to her. Not when he knew damn well he'd be facing his death in a short time, whenever that might be.

By running from his fate twice, he'd tested the gods in a huge way. He was sure they wouldn't let him get away with that a third time. As it was, he was worried about the consequences. He could only imagine what they might be if he tested his gods' mercy again.

And yet, he ached for another hour with Keri. Another day. A week. She was struggling with something, and he wanted to uncover what that issue was, help her overcome it. Force her to, if that was what it took.

An unexpected thought crossed his mind. Perhaps the gods had planned this all along, had intended for him to spend time with Keri? Was it wishful thinking or a true possibility?

Knowing the gods as well as he did, he understood that such a thing would only occur if there was a very significant purpose.

What might he do for this woman, offer her, that no other human being could? A cursed man. One who didn't deserve mercy or kindness at all, but the opposite. What? It had to be something that would require a short time, a few hours or days at most. It couldn't be love.

Again, what could it be?

Still sound asleep, she stirred, her brows drawing down, her smile pulling into a frown. Her breathing grew shallow and fast. She tossed an arm out and whimpered then jerked upright, suddenly wide awake.

Gasping, she glanced at him. Her eyes were wild, full of terror.

"Did you have a nightmare?" he asked.

"Yeah." She nodded, shaking hands scrubbing her face. She sighed. "I don't think I can fall back asleep. I'm pretty sure I don't want to. That was one freaky dream."

"Tell me about it."

She shook her head and tossed the covers off her legs. "No. I'd rather forget it."

He watched her go to the bathroom and shut the door.

Would she call her friend again? He'd heard her earlier, before she'd taken her shower.

Things had changed between them. She didn't look at him the same way anymore. Where there was once open trust and plain desire there was now leery distrust and confusion.

It had to be the way he'd talked to her earlier. The tension between them made him feel sick. His stomach burned like he'd swallowed a gallon of acid. He wished he hadn't needed to say those words. But he did, and he couldn't take them back now. Wouldn't. He'd meant them. In fact, after thinking about the situation, he's even more convinced he'd done the right thing.

He was destined to help this woman. To do more than simply surrender his life. He wondered how long it would take for him to figure out exactly what kind of help he was supposed to lend.

She exited the bathroom scowling, and he guessed she'd had no luck reaching her friend. Or if she had, the friend hadn't told her what she'd wanted to hear.

"Feeling better?" he asked, anticipating the answer.

"Tons," she responded sarcastically.

Damn, he hated the way she looked at him now, talked to him. What would it take to earn her trust back? "Look, about our conversation earlier—"

"Don't worry about it." She climbed back into her bed and jerked the covers over herself. "I'm tired. This whole thing has me all messed up and I'm going back to sleep."

"I can tell you're angry with me. I'd like to talk about it."

"We can talk later, after my nap." She rolled away

from him, leaving him to stare at the back of her head and neck. Even though most of her was covered, he could still see the tension in her body. "Goodnight."

He swallowed a sigh. "I wish I could take you home, since you're obviously unhappy."

"But you can't, since there's some merciless monster hunting me down for no apparent reason. Right?"

"Are you asking if I know why someone wants to kill you?"

Silence.

"Maybe. No." She sighed. "I don't care."

"I don't know anything. Who wants you dead or why. Does that surprise you? Make you feel worse about the situation or better?"

Still facing away from him, she shrugged.

He stood and moved to her bed, sitting on the edge.

She stiffened even more, but she didn't speak, not for several seconds. Finally, when he didn't move away, she glared over her shoulder. "What are you doing?"

"Sitting next to you."

"Obviously."

"Then why ask such an obvious question?"

"I was expecting a less obvious response."

"Hmmm."

She scooted away from him.

"If there was any way to change this situation, you know I would."

"Do I?"

Her sniped comment took him completely by surprise. Yes, something was going on between them. She was upset. That was clear. But the thought that she'd somehow blame him for the killer chasing her had never occurred to him—until now. "What's that supposed to mean? Do you think I want you to be afraid?"

She shrugged again.

"Do you really?" He couldn't stand it anymore, he grabbed her shoulder and pulled hard, forcing her onto her back. She stared at him through enraged, squinty eyes but she didn't say a word. "You honestly believe that?"

Silence.

Her chest rose and fell swiftly, her breathing quick. Her gaze was razor sharp, slicing to his soul. Eyes icy as Siberia in winter.

Insides, his guts twisted. His heart surged to his throat then dropped again. "I swear to you, I never wanted you to be afraid."

Her eyes narrowed even more.

"What makes you think such a thing?"

Finally she opened her mouth to speak.

Desperate to understand, he held his breath and waited. Blood like ice. Heart pounding so loudly in his ears, he could hardly hear anything else.

"Now it's your turn to ask the obvious questions," she snapped.

What the hell?

Confused, he shook his head. "I don't know what you're talking about."

"Come on!" She huffed a loud sigh. "Maybe if you explained why you went to so much trouble to get my attention I might—I emphasize, *might*—decide I don't hate you as much as I do right now."

Huh?

What?

Trouble?

Ohhhh.

She thought he'd...what...? Faked the break-in? And the attack?

He shook his head. Somehow, he had to make her believe this was no joke or ploy. There was a real danger out there, waiting for her to make a wrong move. To keep her safe, he had to have her cooperation and trust.

"I swear I didn't fake anything. There was a man in your apartment, someone I don't know. And that man did attack you, and I had nothing to do with that. Other than if I hadn't stopped him, you would have died." He paused a moment to gauge her reaction. Still, she didn't believe him. "I would have to be a sick bastard to cook up such a scheme."

"Exactly!"

He caught her hands in his and gave them a slight tug, just enough to let her know he meant business. "Listen, I may be a bastard, and some of the things I've told you might seem like utter bullshit, but I would never do such a selfish, underhanded thing. I need you to believe me."

She shook her head, wrenched her hands free from his fists and rolled away from him. "I don't think I can. Not when everything seems to point at your guilt."

"What everything?"

"Just tell me this—when exactly did you call the police to report the attack, and why hasn't anyone asked me to write up a report, describe my attacker, anything?"

"I reported the attack while you were sleeping, after we...that first night, in my apartment. Just like I promised." He paused, snatching the card off the table and fingering a curled corner. "Well, a little later than I promised. I wouldn't let them wake you that night. And we've been on the move since, so he hasn't been by to question you yet. But he has checked out your apartment, has been keeping an eye out for anyone returning to the scene. I've been keeping in contact, letting him know where you are. I have a card. You can call to verify."

Silence.

He stared at her back for several long moments, wondering if he should continue trying to convince her he was speaking the truth. After all, wouldn't it be easier for her to say goodbye later if she believed he was a scoundrel? However, facing the stark truth could come as a horrible shock, and then she'd regret her actions.

Once more, he questioned the reason why he'd been allowed to stay with her for so long. Surely the gods could have interceded by now if they had wished to.

He decided he would try to convince her of the truth. It was his duty. More than that, he *needed* to know she believed him.

Inside, he felt as broken and torn as any wounded warrior on the battlefield. He'd never felt this way about a woman. He stood, paced, struggled to come up with a way to show her he hadn't planned this whole incident as a ruse to get her into his bed. How sad that such a thought had even come to her, but with things as they were between men and women, it was a reasonable conclusion. Hell, when he'd been at his worst, he'd done more than one shameful thing to find his way between a woman's legs.

He had brought very little when they'd left his apartment, just a small bag with the basics. Nothing that would prove he'd lived for centuries. All those things were safely stored at his temporary home, the apartment he'd subleased for a couple of weeks. He had his ring, which he wore at all times. It was very old, but to the average eye looked very much like a modern piece.

No, that wouldn't help.

He hurried to his bag, desperate to find something that might help her believe his seemingly farfetched story. Toothbrush, comb, shorts, T-shirts... No, no, no, no.

He checked the pockets, not sure what he'd find. Razor. Deodorant. Nail clippers.

A miniature?

He couldn't remember packing it, but there it was, the

miniature he'd commissioned in Italy centuries ago. Not expecting it would be finished before he died, he had taken a chance and paid the artist for the piece. And it hadn't been finished. But much to his satisfaction, he learned many years later, when he returned to that same town, that the artist had completed it as promised. The artist had died, but his wife—who was blind—was more than happy to sell it to him.

He kissed it then went to Keri. He could tell from the stiffness in her shoulders that she wasn't sleeping. "I have something to show you."

"I'm trying to sleep."

"You're not sleeping. Because you're upset. This will help you."

She blew out an audible sigh, and he smiled. She truly was a delight. "Fine. What?" She rolled onto her back, crossed her arms over her chest and gave him a glare.

"Hold out your hand."

Her eyes narrowed to slits, but she did as he asked.

He set the locket in her palm.

She glanced at her hand then shot him a questioning glance.

"It's a miniature, painted in Italy during what is now known as the Renaissance. It's all the proof I have that I'm telling the truth."

She fingered the engraved gold frame, the cabochon rubies. "I've never seen one of these up close before." He held his breath as she inspected the setting and scrutinized the painting. She looked at him then took another long look at the miniature. Finally, she closed it and handed it back. "It looks old, and it does resemble you."

"My birthmark." He pointed at the crimson patch of skin just below his earlobe, and the identical mark in the portrait.

Again, she stared at the piece. She turned it over in her hands and checked the back. She flipped it over and looked at the stones embedded in the gold frame, the carving. She ran her fingers over the face of the picture.

"It's real. You could take it to any museum. I have papers back at my apartment to prove its authenticity."

"You expect me to believe you were really—honest to God— alive back during the Renaissance?"

"Really. Yes."

"And before that?"

"I'd like to forget the time we now call the Dark Ages, but yes." Sensing she was struggling with doubt but starting to win the battle, he sat beside her again. She scooted up, reclining against the headboard, her eyes still fixed on that painting. "It's so hard to believe, and I wouldn't know a fake Renaissance painting from a real one..."

"And yet it's so easy to believe the worst."

She shrugged. "I guess I'm jaded."

"No, I think you're pretty normal. I haven't tried telling

anyone about my life before, so I have no idea how most people would react. I have a feeling, though, they'd either call me a liar or write me off as insane."

She pursed her mouth as she lifted her gaze to his. "Every now and then I hear a formality in your speech. And you have a weird accent that I can't pinpoint."

"I think I've acquired some patterns of speech from every place I've been."

"Does that also mean you can speak foreign languages, other than English?"

"Many, including my native tongue, although it's been a very long time. Some of the ancient languages are no longer used and mankind has forgotten them." To illustrate, he said in Hittite, "You are the loveliest creature I have every seen."

Looking a little stunned and wide-eyed, she handed back the miniature. "What was that?"

"Hittite. It's a dead language today. Do you believe me now? I swear to you, I am who I say. But more importantly, I need you to understand that there truly is a killer out there, calculating his next move." He fingered a curled lock of her hair, resting on her shoulder. Her lips parted slightly as her eyes swept over his face. "At first, I thought we'd somehow escaped our fate, outrun the killer and denied the gods their justice. But not anymore. I'm now convinced this is what they want—for us to be together like this. For a little while."

Chapter Seven

Keri tipped her head. "What made you decide that, Talen? Why do you think your gods want us together?"

He could hear the doubt in her voice, the slight clipped edge she gave each word. "I've been abiding the gods' wishes for centuries. There is no chance we could escape for this long without their intervention. For some reason, they are giving us time together."

"But why?"

"I wish I knew." He cupped her cheek. She was so lovely. Soft. Sweet. Tempting. He simply couldn't touch her enough. "I believe it is for your benefit. I must have been sent to you to...I don't know...help you somehow. Heal? Grow? Learn? Or perhaps face something you haven't been able to before."

"Your gods want you to play therapist? Doesn't that seem a little ridiculous?"

He leaned closer, eyes fixed on hers, closer still. Her breath quickened. He felt the warm puffs as she exhaled against his lips.

He sighed and she echoed him.

"Keri," he whispered. He ached to taste her again, to feel her soft body beneath his, to possess her as he had before.

"What Talen?" Her voice was barely audible.

"I'm going to kiss you now." He didn't wait for her response to make good on his promise. The kiss was hard and possessive, a demand, not a question. Tongue, lips and teeth. And she answered with shy swipes of her tongue at first. But as he deepened the kiss, her timidity evaporated. Her strokes grew bolder. Her breath a rough rasp that sounded like the sweetest music in his ears.

"Stop," she murmured, her word saying one thing her voice another.

He cupped her cheeks, holding her face captive, using his hands to change the angle of her head so he could feast upon her as he wished. She rested her hands on his and surrendered control to him.

Ahh, the power. The joy. Breaking away from her mouth, he kissed her face. Everywhere. Then he worked his way to one side, nipped her earlobe, traced the shell of her ear with his tongue, licked a path down the column of her neck, following the visible beat of her pulse to her collarbone.

"T-talen..."

As he kissed, licked and bit, she sighed and whimpered. Her hands finally fell away from his, but they didn't remain still. They skimmed over the swell of his shoulders, down his cotton-covered chest. His nipples hardened to sensitive points under her touch, and blades of warm desire stabbed through his body as she teased them with her fingertips.

Now, this was right. She was on fire for him, yielding and soft, her body pleading for his touch. His body echoed her need, his skin burning for her caress, his blood simmering in his veins, his muscles hardening, tightening as his desire swelled. His cock was so hard, balls so snug, he gritted his teeth.

"Do you honestly believe the gods sent you here for this?" she whispered, one hand gliding down his torso.

"No. I think it's a fringe benefit." He gently forced her down onto her back then pulled the bottom of her shirt up, exposing the concave hollow of her stomach. He bent over, licked. Savored. Lifted the shirt higher until it was gathered on her upper chest. He didn't bother removing it fully. Instead, he unhooked the front clasp on her bra and shoved the garment aside. "I'm going to expose you. All of you. Body. Mind. Soul."

"No, Talen."

The petal-pink nipple stiffened as he blew a soft current of air over it. Simultaneously, the other hardened to the teasing touch of his index finger. So reactive. So perfect. A groan of pleasure swept up his throat.

"I'm going to discover your darkest secrets, your fears, everything you've hidden away."

"Stop. Please."

And a second groan burst from his lips when she clawed her hooked fingers down his chest, the grating, scratching sensation shooting sparks through his bloodstream. In his center, an inferno already burned, the fierce blaze threatening to consume him.

He caught her wrists to stop her, gathered them into one of his fists and forced them up over her head. His free hand plunged to the warm juncture of her thighs. He slid it beneath the elastic waistband of her pajama pants. Moist satiny skin. Nothing felt better.

She made a soft mewling sound and squirmed, tugging at her wrists. "Ohmygod, I'm dying. But you can't..."

"Can't what, Keri?" He fingered her folds, pinching them between his finger and thumb. "Can't touch you like this?"

"No. Can't." She tossed her head from side to side in a show of resistance. But at the same time, her legs slowly pulled apart, giving him easier access to her center.

"You hunger for a man to possess you like this, to surrender." He hooked a finger around the drenched material and pulled sharply. As he hoped, the material gave way.

"No, you're making too much—ohhhhh..." Her stiffened body softened.

Still holding her hands, he shifted positions, turning so he could pin her wrists to the bed while eating her pussy. His burning cock jutted from his groin, angry and demanding, and he longed to feel her full lips circling his girth, her lithe tongue dancing over the tip.

He glanced at her flushed face. Her cheeks were a glorious shade of pink. Her mouth was swollen from his kisses, her lips parted slightly, a temptation he couldn't deny. He straddled her head and pressed the head of his cock against them.

"Suck me."

"No." Despite her denial, she opened her mouth and the head slipped inside. She teased the slit, swirled her tongue round the ridge, suckled gently.

With each pull of her mouth, the flames dancing through his body grew more violent until he was on the verge of collapse. He released her hands, used both of his to drag her knees wide apart and dove between her legs. He found her clit and flickered his tongue over it, quick, sharp strokes. At the same time, he pushed two fingers into her slick passage. The sensation of that moist sheath clamping around his fingers forced a desperate moan from his chest. Still, he clung to his self-control. Until Keri pulled hard on his cock, opening her mouth to take him deep into her throat. A flare blazed down his cock.

"No!" He jerked his rod out of her mouth before sending his come down her throat.

She gave him a fevered glance that had him nearly crumbling to sand as he rolled away from her. He needed a moment, maybe two. Damn, it was hot in here.

"Talen? Is something wrong?"

"Nothing," he said through gritted teeth. Determined not to lose control again, he changed positions, moving completely outside of her reach. He knelt on all fours, his head hovering over the juncture of her thighs.

The air was saturated with the honey-sweet scent of

her juices. He wanted to devour her. His whole body pounded with need. But he resisted. Instead of sinking his cock deep inside, he tasted her, ate her with more patience than he had ever shown before. Despite the flames licking at his skin, the desire blurring his senses and making him dizzy, he took his time.

His tongue danced over her pearl, her flavor filling his mouth, stirring his senses even more.

Beneath his hands, he felt her legs shaking, her skin warming. In his ears, her breathing echoed in a staccato tempo.

"Talen," she whispered, over and over, and he smiled, wondering if she realized she was speaking. Tonight, he wanted to drive her beyond sanity with need, to a place he hadn't been in centuries.

Today would be for his sweet Keri. Every heart-thumping, spine-tingling moment.

Keri swore she was about to die. She'd never known sex could be like this—so much more than a physical experience. Pulses pounding, skin sweating, muscles quivering and nerves tingling. She was too overwhelmed, too lost, to care how lame it was to think this way.

Sex with this man—and this man only—was a whole-being experience. Mind. Body. Soul. Not only was he sending her on a wild physical ride, stroking, licking and kissing her into oblivion, but also whispering sexy promises that sent her mind reeling. And with his eyes, those dark mirrors, he connected with her on an even deeper level.

It was...beyond words.

For the third time, she was shaking all over, muscles tied into excruciating knots, blood churning like molten lava deep within a volcano. Ohhh, she was almost there, that glorious tickly sensation was prickling along every single nerve in her body.

"Please," she whimpered. She could practically see the crest. Closer, yes, closer.

He stopped thrusting his finger into her pussy. Stopped flicking his tongue over her clit.

She wanted to cry but couldn't, not when she knew he'd stroke her, hold her, give her a few minutes to cool off before he'd torment her again. Which he did, the wicked bastard. Twice.

"Have you ever had a man master your body like this?" Talen whispered, his breath tickling her ear. He nipped her neck.

Goose bumps pricked the skin of her arms and shoulders. "No, never. Ohmygod."

"If I had the chance, I'd do this for you every night." He kissed her chin, along her jaw.

She giggled as little bursts of tickly tightness zinged up her neck. "I would die young."

"Oh no you wouldn't." He stopped kissing her and stood. "Condom."

"No. We don't need one. I'm on birth control."

He knelt on the bed and stared with those dark,

torture-filled eyes, his gaze locked to hers. He rested his hands over hers, twining his fingers through hers and settling his hips between her spread legs. "If you belonged to me, I would never let you go."

"But everyone has to die. You couldn't stop that."

He shook his head, and she instantly felt like shit for saying such a stupid thing.

She whispered, "I'm sorry—"

"No, don't. I don't want you to hold back any thought, any words from me. Nothing." His shadowed gaze seemed to drive deep into her soul, the dark shadowy ghosts inside his eyes seeping into her body, swirling through her. She felt like they were tied together by some kind of invisible tether, like their spirits were fused, energy feeding back and forth between them.

He shifted his hips, and the tip of his cock found its way between her folds. She held her breath. Soon, they would be tethered in all ways. In seconds, she hoped.

Torture.

Bliss.

One side of his mouth quirked. His lips parted, but he didn't speak. Something flared in his eyes, and then he rocked his hips back. Surged forward.

Ohhhh yessssss.

His cock was like steel sheathed in satin. He fit her perfectly, filled her completely. He withdrew and slammed forward again, his pelvis smacking against hers. Seated deep inside, he angled his upper body higher, changing the pitch of his entry for a third stroke.

Perfect.

A fourth.

Ecstasy.

A fifth, sixth, seventh.

She lost count after that, completely lost all mental functioning. Instead, she was swallowed up by sensation. She floated on a turbulent sea of hot, pulsing waves. Colors exploded behind her closed eyelids. Sounds blasted at her eardrums. Her skin stung with prickles and burning tingles.

Blind, she reached for him, stroked his shoulder, curled her fingers in his hair, pulled him down, coaxing him to kiss her. How she needed a kiss!

He didn't disappoint her. His mouth crushed hers, a complete possession that was just as absolute as the one below their waists. And while his rod glided in and out of her body, stoking fires throughout her system, his tongue mimicked its motion, making those fires flare with spectacular heat.

He tasted so good, of man and woman and all things carnal. She met his every stab with one of her own. And when he softened the kiss, she followed his lead once again, enjoying the teasing little nips and touches, loving the way her mouth tingled, her heart pounded, her pussy tightened around his prick.

"This time, I'm going to let you come," he whispered against her mouth.

"Thank God."

"But only if you give me something in return."

"Anything."

"Tell me the truth, Keri," he whispered, nipping at her bottom lip. His cock slid out and he let it stay there, the tip barely inside her. "Tell me how much you ache to be possessed by a powerful lover. How you need to surrender to him. To me."

"You're so cruel." She arched her back and pushed her hips forward, trying to take him inside again. Oh, how she hungered for him to possess her. How she ached to surrender to him. Her entire being. Everything. But to say those words? Aloud? She'd never admitted such a thing. Not even to herself. Before now.

"You have no idea how cruel I can be." He pinched her nipple and she moaned.

Ecstasy.

Agony.

They were one and the same at that moment. Sweet torture. That was what it was. How he toyed with her body, not quite touching her as she wanted. Not quite fucking her as she needed. Within ten hammering heartbeats, she was trembling. Within twenty, on the verge of begging.

"Say the words," he whispered. "Keeping them inside doesn't make them any less true. No matter how much you wish it would."

"I...I want a powerful lover."

He caught her wrists and pinned them up over her head. "Want?"

"Desperately."

"That's better." He tipped his hips and his cock slipped a tiny bit deeper.

She groaned and kicked her feet up, trying to wrap them around his waist to force him deeper inside.

He growled, releasing her arms to catch her legs and force them down onto the bed. "Don't move. I am in control. Me." He sat back on his bent legs. His cock slipped out of her and she wanted to cry.

The desire burning inside her didn't ease. Not even a little.

He hooked his hands under her knees and lifted them, forcing them wide apart. "If I could, I would tie your arms and legs, out like this." He pushed on her knees, forcing them out and back so her legs were wide apart. "I would tease you with a dildo until you begged for mercy. Then I'd fuck you slow. In the pussy. In the ass, stopping just before you came. Over and over, I'd take you to the verge of ecstasy. Until you had earned my mercy. Until you had pleased me. Only then would I give you release."

Sounded like heaven. And hell. Both.

"This is only the start of our dance, my sweet. No, it's not a dance." He reached between her legs to tease her labia and clit. "It's a battle. I always win every battle."

She swallowed the comeback that sat on the tip of her tongue, too swept up in the pleasure he was once again stirring in her body to ruin it with a sarcastic comment. It seemed he knew exactly how to touch her. Not too softly. Or too firmly. Just the right amount of pressure. Just the right number of strokes to send her soaring toward completion.

He pushed a finger into her. Two. Ahhh, heavenly. But it wasn't enough. "I know you," he whispered. "I can read every movement. Every shudder and sigh." He twisted his wrist, hooking his fingers to stroke her G-spot and she cried out. It felt so amazing she was ready to do anything he asked. "Tell me."

She rocked her head from side to side. "Talen, please."

"I promise I will torment you until you break." A second later, he jerked his fingers away, about two seconds before she came.

Bastard!

A shudder raced down her spine. He was so right. She did crave a lover who knew how to take control. But not in a scary way. In this way. "I..."

"Yes, Keri."

"I need you to take control. I need to surrender."

"Yes, Keri." He pushed her knees back and entered her swiftly, his cock gliding home. In. Out. His thrusts were just right. The rhythm she needed. Neither too hard nor too soft.

In short order, she was soaring again, sensations blending into an intoxicating, magical blur. She became lost in it, drowning in carnal pleasure.

"Now, surrender. Come." He flicked a fingertip over

her sensitive clit and colors burst behind her closed eyelids. A tingling, electrical charge buzzed up to her scalp and down to the soles of her feet. And then whoosh, her body spasmed. It was the kind of orgasm that left her breathless, quivering, clinging to Talen's sweat-slicked body.

What this man did to her.

For her.

Keri woke up alone. Sore, in a good way. Starving. And rumpled. Sitting up, she noticed the piece of paper sitting on the nightstand.

He had the most unusual handwriting. Difficult to read, slanted, with crisp strokes and little flourishes on the capital letters that made her think of old handwritten documents like the Declaration of Independence.

My Angel,

Went for food. Be back as soon as I can. Love, Talen.

Love.

A dorky smile plastered on her face, she hurried to the bathroom to get cleaned up. The long, hot shower felt great, water pounding on achy muscles, the fragrance of lavender filling the steamy room. She came out a little while later, hair and makeup done, ready to face whatever the day might bring.

Talen hadn't returned yet.

A little flare of worry crept up her spine, but she shoved it aside. Nobody was trying to kill him, she reasoned. They were after her. So, he was safe—safer away from her than with her.

Gosh, this whole thing was overwhelming, when she took the time to really think about it. Yesterday, he had finally convinced her he was telling the truth. Still, it was hard to accept the truth, to fully comprehend what it meant.

He died. Over and over again. He'd done so for thousands of years. Suffered one horrific, violent and painful death after another.

She couldn't imagine.

This man. Talen. The guy who stroked her so sweetly and tormented her so thoroughly put himself in the proverbial line of fire over and over again. And for strangers, no less.

He was a remarkable man. The sacrifice.

When she tried to step into his shoes, she could imagine how lonely he had to be. Waking up in a strange place and then dying before he was able to make any friends, form any bonds with anyone.

To suffer in such isolation. It was a wonder he wasn't insane.

If some sort of ancient beings were behind this, if it truly was a curse, they were beyond cruel to assign such a punishment to any human being. People needed other people. Some form of a connection. Friendship. Love. Whatever form it took. To deny anyone such a basic need was heartless.

And from what she'd seen, Talen was the last man on earth who deserved such punishment.

Pffft to those mean, merciless gods of his!

She made a point of not speaking any of her thoughts aloud, hoping his gods couldn't know her thoughts, like the God she'd always *thought* she believed in.

She was ashamed to admit this experience had shaken her faith in God. One God. Many gods. Which could it be? Of course, she hadn't attended church in a couple of years, her Bible was collecting dust and she hadn't prayed in ages. Looking at it from an objective viewpoint, her faith hadn't been all that strong, anyway.

She still wondered what this meant, when it came to all those people who truly believed there was only one God. It couldn't be both—Talen's ancient gods couldn't exist, if what she understood about the bible was true.

Something deep to think about. But not now.

She flopped onto the bed, staring at the small pile of personal items Talen had set on top of the dresser. Another look at that tiny painted portrait would be nice. She'd been absolutely blown away by the skill the artist had used in creating it. Such minute detail. Itty-bitty brushstrokes.

Keri's mother had been an artist, a remarkably talented one. Sadly, like many, her mother had also been a little touched, not quite right but not insane enough to warrant any medical intervention. Regardless, Keri had learned to appreciate art in its many forms.

This form was fascinating.

She plucked up the locket and stared at the portrait, marveling at the artist's talent. So many times, she'd tried to paint. Some of her paintings were reasonably well done, at least to the average eye. But not to hers. They'd always lacked something.

An idea slowly formed in her head.

How many times had Talen received a gift? Birthday. Christmas, whatever. Wasn't he deserving? How sad, that his life's most precious possessions could fit in his pocket.

A present. For a man who repeatedly gave the most precious gift of all.

It wouldn't be an oil painting, but it was something, a very special kind of present that only she could give.

She found a notepad and pen on the desk. And with one goal in mind, she began to sketch.

Chapter Eight

Talen's heart was in his throat, and it wasn't because he was preparing himself to die again. He'd learned a long time ago to face death calmly. This was far more nerve-racking than death.

He was about to do something he hadn't done in so long he honestly couldn't remember the last time. He was about to give Keri a present.

It wasn't so much that the gift was expensive. It was, but because his gods had determined that a lack of currency would threaten their goals, he had an inexhaustible source of money. Every morning, his pockets were full, no matter how much he spent the day before. Cash. In the local government's currency. On hand whenever he needed.

Instead, it was the intimacy of the act that made it so scary. And what a rejection would mean—utter destruction, truthfully. He felt sick, just imagining her shaking her head, refusing the present he'd struggled so long to select.

His shopping spree had kept him away from her for a lot longer than he would have liked, but he'd known the whole time that her killer hadn't yet located her. His neck was blessedly burn-free. Thus, the only risk he'd taken by being gone for so long was losing precious time with her.

That was bad enough.

Which was why he couldn't stand on this side of the door any longer, even if he was so nervous he swore his knees were about to give. He slid the key card into the lock, pulled it out. The lock clicked and he opened the door.

She was standing beside the bed, her hands hidden behind her back, a strained look on her face. "Talen."

"Keri? Is something wrong?" His heart lurched, and he slapped his hand over his neck, even though he didn't feel any stinging there. He dumped the bag onto the bed and rushed to her, pulling her into his arms and crushing her body against his.

Oh, how perfectly she fit there, in his embrace, her body conforming to his.

Slipping her arms around his waist, she shook her head. "No, no. Nothing's wrong. I was just..."

He felt her tipping her head back, and he reluctantly loosened his hold to allow himself to meet her gaze.

She said, "I...feel kind of stupid...I made you something."

"You did what?" The strangest sensation buzzed through his insides, warming him and making him feel electrified. His eyes started burning, and he realized what that sensation meant.

True, profound joy. It had been so long, he'd forgotten what it felt like.

He felt alive, so energized, he could leap into the air, conquer any hurdle, defeat any foe. A gift? His sweet Keri had wanted to give him a gift.

She was watching him closely, her gaze marked with reluctance, confusion. "Are you angry?"

"No, no. I'm simply...I don't know what to say. No one has shown me any sort of kindness in such a long time. But you..." He cupped her cheek, dragged his thumb over her plump lower lip. "Whatever the gods had in mind when they brought you to me, I'm afraid I don't quite know how to react."

The corners of her mouth curled into a soft smile, and something sweet sparkled in her eyes. "Maybe you'd better wait to decide how to react until after you see what it is. Really, it's not much. I mean, I couldn't go anywhere, and I don't have anything with me."

He nearly wept when she released him. He took her cue, even though it was the last thing he wanted to do, and let his arms fall to his sides.

His body let him know what a foolish act that had been.

But then she handed him a rolled-up piece of paper, tied with a ribbon. "Just promise me you won't laugh." She clapped her hands over her mouth when he took it from her.

"I promise." He tugged on the bow and unrolled the paper, and his breath caught in his throat.

He had never seen such a remarkable likeness of himself, particularly in the eyes. It was so striking he couldn't stop staring at it. "How? Where?"

"I drew it."

Awestruck, he looked at the picture again. "But I didn't sit for you."

"I drew it from memory, although I admit I used the miniature as a reference."

"And I wasn't gone very long."

Her cheeks pinked. He liked that shade. He kissed one. Her skin was warm, and so soft.

She shrugged. "I know I'm not Rembrandt or anything, but I've always liked to draw."

"You don't give yourself enough credit. You clearly have a gift. Have you had any training?"

"None. I quit taking art classes in high school."

He shook his head, still not sure what to say, do. His own gift for her was sitting in the bag, not forgotten. But still, he felt out of sorts. A simple thank-you seemed so inadequate, especially since he was the last man who deserved a gift from anyone, particularly such an amazing woman as Keri.

There was one big problem. He sensed she was beginning to care about him. More than she should. More than he'd ever wanted her to. Which meant she was going to be hurt when he died.

"Tell me you don't hate it." She sounded worried.

"No! I don't hate it. It's amazing, and I'm touched that

139

you thought to do such a thing. This means more than I could even try to explain. But you shouldn't have."

"Why?"

It was time to pull back, put some distance between them. This was his fault. He'd convinced himself this was what the gods had wanted. What a fool he'd been! Of course, the gods didn't want him to get close to this woman or any other.

The bottom line was he'd pushed her, dragging her into an intimacy she wasn't ready for, and now that he had what he'd been wanting, the selfish bastard he was, he felt like hell. "I'm not the man you think I am, and I don't deserve anything."

"No, please don't say that." She clapped her hand over his mouth. Tears gathered in her eyes, that shimmering wetness like acid, burning his insides. Shaking her head, she let her hand fall from his mouth. "You are a brave, thoughtful, amazing man. A better man than I've ever met."

"I'm a selfish ass and a fool."

"Fool? No." She dragged her forefingers along her bottom lashes, sniffled.

Damn, how he hated to see her cry. But better for her to weep now, when he could still hold her, give her some comfort, than later when she'd be alone.

"I pushed and pushed for you to open up, thinking the gods had sent me to you for some reason. But in making you open up, I've made you vulnerable. And I can't stand the thought that you'll be hurt when I die." A hot prick stung the back of his neck, and without thinking, he smacked his hand over the painful spot.

Keri's eyes widened.

"Keri."

A wild expression he couldn't name swept over her face. She stabbed an index finger at his neck. "He's back? He found us." She rushed to the door and snapped the bolt in place. "It's too soon. Not yet, please not yet." She stood on tiptoes, hands flattened against the door, checking the peephole.

"Keri!" He rushed up behind her and roughly pulled her around to face him.

"It's not fair, Talen." Tears weren't just dripping from her eyes now, they were streaming, and he felt like a sword had been thrust in his gut and twisted. "I never wanted to let anyone get close to me. And now that I've opened up a little, the one person I took a chance with is going to die. Right in front of my eyes." She jerked away from him, pounded her fists against his chest. "Fuckfuckfuck! It's so fucking unfair." Her fury building before his eyes, she swung back and slapped him on the upper arm.

The sting felt good. Right. He deserved that strike and so many more.

She threw her hand back to deliver a second blow, and he did nothing to stop her. After all, she was right, and he'd been wrong, terribly wrong for asking her for the intimacy she'd given him. It was like he'd become addicted. To her. No, to the feeling of being close to her.

141

He'd let his addiction take over. Stopped thinking.

Again, it was no wonder he was cursed. After all these years, decades, centuries, he was still thinking only of himself.

He reached for the door. "I'll end this right now. That way you won't hurt anymore."

"No." She knocked his arm aside. "Don't you get it? I will hurt. I'll hurt as much now as I would three hours from now. Three days. Three weeks. It's too late, Talen. I thought it was impossible to fall in love with a stranger, but that's exactly what I'm doing. I'm fucking falling in love with you."

Her words hurt him more than a blade through the chest, a bullet through the skull, being crushed beneath a bus. "No."

She pounded on his chest again, fingers curled into tight fists, each blow punctuating three words. "Yes. I. Am!"

He caught her wrists as they sailed toward his body for a fourth. "Keri. Listen to me." He waited until her gaze met his before continuing. "You are not falling in love with me. You can't. For one thing, I don't deserve your love. I don't deserve anyone's love."

"What makes you so sure of that?"

"Because I know myself a whole helluva lot better than you know me."

They stood silent for several agonizing moments, the air around them so charged up with electricity, it was superheated, thick and heavy.

"I've never felt this way about anyone before." Her eyes were so full of pain, he nearly dropped to his knees.

"Maybe it's because of the fear," he reasoned. "People who face tragedy tend to develop unnatural bonds with each other. I should have thought of that..." He pulled her to him, wrapped his arms around her slender form and held her tightly. She trembled as she nestled close, tucking her head beneath his chin and breathing so heavily he could hear every inhalation and exhalation. "Forgive me, Keri. I'm so fucking selfish." Again, he found himself rubbing at the stinging skin at his nape.

She pushed away from him, staggering backward. "We have to leave."

"No, it's time to say goodbye. I can't stand—"

"No!" She whirled around and ran into the bathroom and slammed the door.

Determined to help her somehow face the inevitable, he raced after her, halting outside the bathroom door. "Keri, I was wrong to get this close to you, and an idiot for convincing myself that this was the gods' divine plan for you."

"We have to leave." The door flew open. Inside the bathroom, Keri rushed around, scooping up her personal possessions and cramming them into her overnight bag.

She wasn't listening.

Once she had her belongings gathered, she jerked the bag's strap over her shoulder and charged toward him, her gaze focused on his face.

He stopped her, wrapped his fingers around both her

upper arms. "Keri, we can't keep running. And it'll be better facing this now than later, when the pain will be even greater."

"No, Talen. You were right. Those fucking gods of yours are asses, and we need to defy them as many times as it takes. I'm giving you a gift. Don't you see that? Over and above the drawing, I'm giving you something much more valuable—hope, happiness, my heart."

He shook his head. "I can't accept your gifts."

"Yes you can. You have to." Teeth gritted, eyes red, she shoved his chest. "You can't just let it happen. Fight, dammit! If you won't fight for yourself, fight for me."

He released her, lurched backward.

"Maybe that's why you've never broken the curse. Have you thought about that? Could it be because you've never had the guts to tell those fucking bastards that you've had enough?"

Damn, he felt like his insides had been beaten beneath the hooves of a dozen horses. He wanted to apologize again, but he knew his words would fall on deaf ears. Keri was too lost in panic to hear anything he would say.

The burning at his nape intensified. Time was short. He swung around.

She was jamming her clothing into the bag as if her life was in jeopardy. "Come on, Talen. We've ditched him twice already, we can do it again."

"Maybe. But sooner or later we will run out of time. He will catch us. The gods will make sure of it. They will lead him to us." Inside, he screamed, cursed, cussed, fumed. Outside, he sighed, gathered the few belongings he had brought with him, swept up Keri's drawing, tucked it into the bag of food he'd forgotten about, and followed her toward the door.

He would not touch her again.

He would not kiss her again.

He would not permit himself any pleasure whatever.

What he would do was prepare her for what had to occur.

If the gods would permit him. And if—somehow—he was able to find the strength to deny his body what it demanded.

Outside they ran, to the elevator. They rushed through the lobby and out into a bright, warm morning. Birds chirped. A soft breeze carried the scents of freshly mown grass and car exhaust to his nose. He glanced around, nervous, unsure if they'd get away this time.

The burning at his nape was stronger than ever. The killer was close, watching them, likely. He turned to Keri, offered his hand. She smiled through her tears, placed her hand in his and followed his lead as he ran.

Chapter Nine

Keri couldn't believe she'd actually said those words aloud, *I'm falling in love with you.* Until she'd spoken them, she hadn't believed them. After all, she didn't fall in love. At least, she hadn't before.

This man...he was so different, so strong and commanding and special. Somehow he'd snuck right past her defenses and captured her heart without her even realizing it. Until it was too late.

Now, all she could think about was finding a way to escape his curse. Any doubt she'd had about him had evaporated, and she was now fully convinced he was indeed destined to die. For her.

She simply couldn't let that happen.

She needed to get some information. A computer. The internet. That was where she always turned when she had a question or needed facts.

Her friend was out of town for a few more days.

She had a computer.

She lived close by.

And although Keri didn't have a key, she knew how to

get into the house without one.

"This way!" She stopped, turned and headed back in the direction from which they'd come. "It's only a mile or so."

"What is?" Talen shifted the paper bag he held in his arms.

"A friend's house. We can stay there. She won't mind." Slightly breathless from the run-walk pace she was keeping, she tightened her hold on Talen's hand. "How's your neck?"

"Burning like hell and getting worse."

"Shit." Thinking quickly, she took a turn down a side street, a meandering, narrow road that curved through a subdivision full of middle-class brick colonials. "Better?"

A short distance away, the screech of tires echoed, and a chill shot up her spine. She stopped beside a towering oak to catch her breath and think.

Talen nodded. "Better, yes. A little."

"Do you think those squealing tires belonged to our killer?"

"It's possible."

"But he's not following us?"

He fingered his neck. "No. Not right now. But he isn't gone either. He's looking for us, circling around the hotel maybe."

Those words were enough to kick her fanny into high gear. She took a look around, glanced longingly at the car sitting in a driveway. "A car would sure come in handy right now."

"I can get us one."

"You can? How? And why didn't you say something sooner?"

He shrugged, slowing to a stroll as they neared a silver Isuzu. "Because you never mentioned it." He handed her the grocery bag.

"So, how's this work? Do you make a wish or something, and it magically appears?"

He laughed. "You're funny." He squatted next to the car.

She mirrored him. "Then what...hey, what are you doing?"

"Getting us a car. It's unlocked. And I saw someone do this in a movie once..."

"Oh no! I didn't expect you to steal one."

He opened the door and slipped into the driver's seat. "You were joking about the magic, right?"

"No I wasn't! Get out of there!"

"But you said you wanted a car."

"Not that bad."

"Very well then." He exited the vehicle and quietly shut the door, and she shoved the bag into his arms before making tracks for the end of the street. She hoped and prayed no one saw that stunt. Ohmygod, she'd almost become an accessory to grand theft auto or whatever it was called.

A few minutes later, and a couple blocks away from

the house with the almost-stolen car, she allowed herself to slow down. Only a smidge, from a jog to a race-walk. Breathless, and feeling like her lungs were on fire, she asked, "How's your neck now?"

"Not too bad," he responded, not sounding at all winded.

"Still stinging?"

"Slightly. He's not giving up easily."

"Then he wants me dead badly." Too tired to go on, she hurried around the back of a large delivery van, bent over at the waist and dragged in a few much-needed deep breaths. She tipped her head to look up at Talen. "I still don't understand why anyone would want to kill me. I haven't done anything to anyone. Well, except for that one time when I called someone a name on an online forum. She—if it truly was a she, I have my doubts—was a freak and an ass. She gave my email address to a bunch of spammers, stole my identity and posted a bunch of stuff on some forums. More or less made me look like a psycho. Do you think she, he, whoever, made good on her threat to come looking for me?"

"I honestly don't know."

She straightened up. "I have an idea. What if we figured out who it is? We could stop her—without your having to die..."

"I've never been able to change a victim's fate."

"Have you tried before?"

"Only once, before I met you."

"It didn't work."

"No."

After a long stretch of silence, she asked, "Did this person mean something to you? The one you tried to fight the curse for?"

"They all did."

That was so hard for her to understand. Strangers, hundreds or thousands of them, they all meant something to him?

She wasn't exactly the world's biggest bitch, but she wasn't out to make friends with every stranger she passed. She was somewhere in between, or so she liked to think. She would never feel the way Talen did about strangers. People she would never see again.

On the other hand, these were people he knew were about to die. She knew some doctors and nurses became emotional about trauma victims they've worked on in the hospital. Police and firefighters too. It could be the same kind of thing.

Okay, she supposed it was somewhat understandable.

She started walking again, taking a cue from Talen. He was rubbing his neck. "Then she was special like all the rest of us?"

"What makes you think it was a woman?"

"Just a guess."

After a few seconds, he said, "You are more special than the rest, even her."

Her heart lurched and she found herself wanting to lighten things up. "That's just because we had sex."

"I had sex with her too."

And how many others? Her insides twisted, and she realized she was jealous. That was a total shock.

"Nobody else," he said as if he'd read her mind. He caught her hand in his empty one, threaded his fingers through hers.

That meant he'd had sex with two people. In how many years?

"She was a marchioness, a member of Henry VIII's court and a lady in waiting to Her Majesty Queen Anne."

"Anne? The Anne Boleyn? That was...what? The 1500s. That's a long time to wait for sex."

"Yes, it is. After she died, I vowed to never again become acquainted with another victim. I wished to spare them the horror of watching me die for them."

"But not me?"

"That's why I begged your forgiveness. I found myself..." he dropped the bag, crushed her against a tree and thrust his arms forward, trapping her between them, "...bewitched."

She met his gaze, saw the fire in his eyes and wished she could stir it up a little more. But not now. Not with a killer chasing them. "I'm no witch."

"So you say." He bent his elbows and angled lower, until his face was right there, in front of hers and their mouths were almost touching. "I say you are and you've ensnared me with your charms." He brushed his mouth over hers. "I don't wish to be freed, Keri. Ever."

"And I don't wish to free you," she admitted, shocking herself. She stared at him for a moment, her gaze taking in every detail of his features, wishing she could burn them into her memory. Wishing she wouldn't have to face a future without seeing that face.

Oh God, she was the one who was ensnared, bewitched, bedeviled, whatever!

She wasn't acting like herself, or thinking like herself, or even feeling like herself. It was as if this man had somehow drawn someone else out of her. A someone who wasn't afraid to feel certain things, to take chances and face her insecurities.

She wasn't sure if she liked what was happening. "Um, we better get moving before that killer finds us again." She shoved at his chest. "It isn't much farther."

As he bent to retrieve the bag, he flinched, his face suddenly a mask of pain. She spun around, catching sight of a car taking the corner so fast its tires shrieked.

She jerked back around, shouting, "The killer?"

He nodded.

Instinct kicked in. She grabbed Talen's hand and sprinted toward a house.

Safety. Hide.

She heard the car's engine behind them. Too close. What if he had a gun? A moving target was harder to hit. Keep running. She raced around the side of a red brick ranch, legs burning, lungs on fire. Dead end. Locked gate. Dammit!

Terrified, she glanced over her shoulder. The car was parked on the street.

She grabbed the wooden gate and shook it. Fumbled with the latch. "Talen!"

He reached over the top and unhooked it from the back, the gate swung open just as the pounding sound of footfalls rounded the corner behind them.

Too close! She ran harder, pushing her legs to go as fast as they could. She felt lightheaded, like she was about to pass out. Her legs hurt so badly, yet she couldn't slow down. Across a grassy backyard, she dashed. Around a wooden play structure with bright colored swings and slides. At the rear, she saw another gate. Talen was behind her. She heard him following as she literally slammed into the gate at the rear of the yard. She flipped the latch and shoved the gate open.

A park. Wide open field. Not good. She raced toward a small copse of trees along one side, hoping their pursuer might lose her in there.

But before she reached it, her exhausted muscles gave way. Her knees turned to jelly, and down she went. She hit the ground hard, scrambled back to her feet and tried to start running again, but someone caught her from behind, yanking her backward. Down she went. On her back.

It was him—the man from her apartment.

"No, please," she begged, too focused on him to try to

find Talen. Where'd he go? "Why?"

The man didn't speak, just thrust a hand into a worn denim jacket. Before he withdrew it, he was suddenly thrown off her by one red-faced Talen. While she rolled over and jumped to her feet, the two men fought furiously. Talen got in a good punch but the killer returned in kind. And before she had exhaled, both men were bloody and battered.

Finally, Talen threw a punch that had to have broken a few bones. The killer crumpled to the ground, and she snatched up the grocery bag and was on the run again, with Talen at her side. They raced through the park then took a roundabout route through the subdivision, keeping out of sight as much as possible.

She glanced at the sky as she jogged. It couldn't be past ten o'clock, and so much had happened already today. What would the rest of the day hold?

She hoped anyone's death wouldn't be a part of today's festivities. Silent, lost in her thoughts, she led Talen to her friend's house. As expected, the front door was locked. Same with the garage and French doors in the back of the house.

But, as usual, the bedroom window's lock was disengaged and the window didn't fully close. They were inside, safe and sound, within minutes.

At last, Keri could breathe easier.

When Talen excused himself to use the bathroom to clean up, Keri started pulling things out of the grocery bag he'd been carrying.

She found a long, narrow velvet-covered jewelry box at the very bottom, hidden beneath a plastic carton of fruit. Inside, she found a beautiful choker. Two rows of sparkling red stones comprised the wide band. From the center hung an amulet of some kind, fashioned out of silver metal and studded with more red stones.

Breathtaking, even if the stones were glass. They sure were gorgeous, for fakes.

At the sound of Talen's approaching footsteps, she laid the choker in the box, but she didn't have it closed before he entered the room.

She knew because he said, "Oh."

"I found it in the bottom of the bag," she explained, feeling as though she'd been caught with her hand in the cookie jar. The box's hinged top snapped when she closed the lid. Awkwardly, she handed the box to him. "I'm sorry. I shouldn't have opened it."

"It's okay." He waved a hand, indicating she should keep it. "It's for you. I was hoping to pick the right time to give it to you, but, well, I guess this is it. Eh?"

"You bought me a present? That's very sweet." She ran a fingertip over the top of the box then opened it again, this time noticing the name printed in gold letters on the box's satin-lined top. Exquisite Jewelers. Specializing in custom-designed fine jewelry since 1961.

Something hard wedged itself in her throat.

She'd heard of that place. It was a small shop tucked between Kroger grocery store and a Coney Island restaurant, and they sold uber-expensive stuff. Platinum and diamonds, natural rubies and emeralds. She'd wandered in there once. Didn't stay long.

Nobody had ever bought her such a nice gift. She didn't want to guess how much something like this must have cost.

One thing was for certain—nothing came free. Everything she'd ever possessed had cost her in some way, even if she hadn't paid money for it. Gosh, what sort of strings would be attached to a present that had to have cost as much as her car? Freaking steel chains? Then again, what sort of strings could a man who was about to die require?

"Talen, I don't know what to say." Why would he do such a thing? He'd purchased it before he'd known about her gift to him—which now looked like a kid had made it in kindergarten, compared to his.

"Thank you would be fine." Looking a smidgen stiff, he grabbed a foam carryout box and flipped the top.

"Sure, yes. I mean, thank you. But, Talen, it's so expensive."

His gaze snapped to hers. Intense. Dark. "Do you like it, Keri?"

It was a question, and yet she heard something else in his voice. Fear? Doubt? What was he feeling?

"It's absolutely beautiful."

"But you can't accept it." This time, it wasn't a question.

"Nobody gives presents to people they hardly know.

Not for no reason."

"I die for strangers, Keri."

Good point.

"And I do not—would not, even if I could—ask for anything in return."

She was so not used to such thinking. People in her world never did anything for anyone, not without some kind of expectation. That included herself. Which made her realize that her gift had been more or less her way of paying Talen for what he would do later. It was such a piddly price to pay, actually a slap in the face when she thought about it.

A drawing that had taken her less than an hour, in exchange for his acceptance of the suffering and death that had been meant for her.

She brushed the pad of her thumb over the lid, realizing she would not be able to wear that choker after he was dead, not without feeling like she'd had her insides squeezed in a vise. "You've already given me enough." She tried to hand it back to him, but he refused to accept it. So instead, she set it on the counter, between the foam box loaded with some kind of omelet and another one cram-packed with buttered toast.

Silently, her thoughts whirring through her head like a swarm of insects, she filled a plate with food and warmed it in the microwave. Talen was sitting at the table, his hands resting on either side of his plate and a distant look on his face. He was staring at something. She glanced over her shoulder but saw nothing.

Her plate clacked on the table's glass top—ceramic striking glass. Another loud clatter echoed through the room when she set down her silverware. Talen bounded to his feet when she dragged her chair out to sit and quickly grabbed at the chair's back to push it in as she lowered into the seat.

"Thanks," she murmured.

He responded with a strained smile that told her something was wrong. That sense grew increasingly pronounced as they ate. He said nothing. Not a single word. She found herself tempted to chatter about nothing and everything, just to fill the uncomfortable silence.

If she hadn't been absolutely starving, she would have had a terrible time eating. Now that she'd stuffed herself full of eggs, fruit and toast, however, she was feeling like she'd swallowed a lump of concrete. Her chest burned too. It was a terrible feeling, one she couldn't endure for another minute.

After putting her dirty dishes in the dishwasher, she turned to Talen, who was dropping the empty carryout cartons in the trash. "Talen?"

"Hmm?"

"Are you upset with me?"

"No."

"You've grown so quiet."

"I guess I ran out of things to say."

That was such a guy thing.

"No, it's more than that. I can tell." When he didn't

respond, she added, "Is it because I didn't want to accept the gift you bought?"

He shrugged, and she realized, shockingly, that the shadows she'd seen in his eyes weren't from doubt or fear, but hurt.

"I can't accept that choker from you because it's too expensive, Talen, not because it came from you. That was the most generous, kindest thing anyone has ever done for me, but you're already giving me a precious gift and..." Whatever words she'd wanted to say slipped from her mind, and she was left floundering, lost for words, her face warming.

He was standing there, arms crossed over his chest looking so strong and yet vulnerable at the same time. A man who had the power to do God only knew. Now he'd been figuratively brought to his knees. By her words. Mind blowing.

She'd never felt so powerful yet so conflicted.

How could she make him understand? Especially when she herself didn't fully understand.

He rubbed the back of his neck.

"Has the killer found us already?"

"No. We're safe. At least for now." His gaze met hers. "I'd like to take a shower now. Wash off the rest of the dirt and blood."

"Sure." She brushed past him, her body reacting to his nearness with a surge of heat. "This way. I'll show you where everything is." She paused, even though she knew lingering in that position—with him standing so close—

would make her melt. "Thank you for getting breakfast."

He crowded her and something flickered in his eyes. A dark spark that ignited a blaze in her body. "You're welcome." He pinched her chin between his thumb and forefinger, lifting it until her gaze met his. "Maybe you'd like to take a shower with me."

That was no question. It was a challenge, the kind she didn't have the strength or willpower to back away from.

Chapter Ten

Things sure did happen fast when one was in the same room with Talen. Less than a dozen stuttering heartbeats ago, Keri had been standing in a hallway, motioning toward the bathroom at the end of the corridor. Now she was bouncing down said hallway, flung over the shoulder of a man who made her knees wobble and her heart bang against her ribcage. And a pair of hands that did the most amazing, naughty things to her body was holding her. One rested on her fanny. The other gripped her leg, strong fingers curled around her ankle.

Not only did she feel giddy and weightless but also unbelievably aroused. Again. She couldn't ever remember being so freaking horny. This was insanity.

Wicked. Thrilling. Naughty craziness.

Down the hallway her captor glided, his body moving with a strength and fluid grace that reminded her of a jungle cat. The bathroom door was open so he strolled inside, cranked on the shower, then, finally, set her on her feet.

She reached for him, catching his arms to steady herself. She glanced up.

Total headrush.

He smiled.

She practically fell over. It was odd, how her body reacted to him. So intensely it was almost violent, not quite painful but verging on agony. All it took for her to fall apart was a look from him. That particular look, where one side of his mouth was curled up into a lopsided smile and feral hunger flickered in his dark eyes. He made her feel feminine, attractive, sexy, and a little vulnerable, but in a very good way.

Steam wafted over the top of the glass shower door, creating a magical, sultry world of damp heat. Her skin felt hot and cold at the same time, prickly and uber-sensitive.

His gaze slowly wandered down her body. He didn't move, didn't speak, just stood there, hard and hot and tempting, and looked at her as if he was trying to decide what to do with her next.

She knew what she wanted him to do with her. Just like she knew what she wanted to do with him.

She stood there, battling silently between the urge to throw herself at him, or turn tail and run away. Something. It was strange just staying put, not moving, not doing anything.

Weird but also really sexy.

She felt like he was holding her captive. Not with ropes. Or with chains. But with his eyes. And much to her shock, she liked the way she felt right now, despite the sense of powerlessness.

There were a lot of scenarios she'd secretly fantasized about. Movie scenes that had curled her hair. Television series that had inspired her to whip out the battery-operated devices and put them to use. Books that made her dream about things she'd never in a million years consider trying.

But not once had she ever thought any kind of submission was sexy. Until now.

Whether she wanted to admit it or not, she was standing there, still as a statue, because he had told her to. With his eyes. And that little bit of power she'd handed him gave her such a rush, the juices were seeping from her pussy so hot and fast the insides of her thighs were slick.

"Take off your clothes," he commanded.

She complied, her gaze fixed to his as she stripped off each piece. With every inch of skin she exposed, the fire in his eyes grew darker and more violent. It was the most amazing sight.

Before she realized it, she was completely nude, trembling.

"You're so fucking beautiful," he murmured, his gaze returning to her face. He walked a slow circle around her, and she literally felt him as he moved out of her peripheral vision. Her skin zapped and stung. She heard the whir of the vanity drawer open. Bottles and jars rattle. The pop of a lid being opened. "Your face. Your shoulders." He now stood directly behind her. A lubricated fingertip traced the slope of her shoulder blade, and a quiver raced down her spine. "Your back. Your ass." That finger followed her spine, leaving a path or goose pumps behind. Down it went, to the dip between her ass cheeks.

She struggled to stand. Her breathing had grown so fast and deep, it sounded like she'd just sprinted a marathon. The breathy echo bounced off the tile and glass, making it that much louder.

"Have you ever taken a man here?" His finger slid deeper, teased her anus.

"No. Never." She'd always been too afraid to let a man try. She'd seen it in porn movies. Pictures. It looked way too painful to even think about.

Until now.

Ohmygod, how amazing it felt to have that fingertip teasing, dipping into her hole. Would it be that much more amazing if it was his cock? Or pure hell?

She needed to find out.

He groaned. "You see how unkind you are? How cruel, to give me so many sweet gifts, like this, and refuse mine." His finger slowly worked deeper into her ass as she fought to relax, suddenly desperate to be filled.

"I'm not trying..."

"You don't have to." He thrust his finger deeper, and she practically fell to her knees. As if he sensed her legs were about to give out, he slid his other hand around her waist. Fingers splayed over her lower stomach while his arm supported her weight.

Now, she was even more powerless, completely at his mercy. He held her firmly. In place. While he worked a second lubricated finger into her anus.

The sensitive skin burned. She tightened, her body fighting against the invasion. The hand on her stomach slid lower, over her mound, between her legs. He found her clit.

"You want me to take you like this. You crave a powerful lover. I sensed it the moment I saw you."

"How?" she heard herself whisper.

"You have the eyes of a submissive. The heart of one too. And your body...mmmmmm..." The second finger slipped past the tight ring of muscles and she was full. Wonderfully, exquisitely full. "It hungers for the chance to surrender to a strong lover."

She could buy that right now.

He gently moved his fingers inside her, scissoring them to test her and she enjoyed every second. More than she ever would have guessed. Fleeting flickering blazes danced through her body. This was such a mind-blowing moment, erotic. In a dark, slightly unnerving way. Sensual.

He pulled his fingers out, and she whimpered, turning to face him. He pulled her close, cupped her ass. "Time to stop. We're going to run out of hot water. After you wash me, then you will receive what you've been waiting for."

She would never—ever!—admit it aloud, but the way he'd said that part about washing him made her all quivery and hot inside. Even more than his promise to deliver what she was waiting for.

Why did a command from this man seem so sexy when any other man making such a bold suggestion would produce icicles?

No time to ponder such insignificant things. She was being pushed gently under a stream of hot water. The beat of the drops on her back and head felt wonderful. So did the sensation of Talen's hands gliding over her head and shoulders as he gathered her wet hair in his fist and tugged.

He forced her around until she faced the spray. Now he stood behind her, one hand still knotted in her hair, the other sliding down her side, fingers pressing into her skin. "You amaze me. In so many ways. Your body, of course. But also your mind. Your spirit. Your soul." He tugged on her hair, forcing her to tip her head back and to one side. And then, taking advantage of his position, he looped his arm around her waist, dragging her against him. His hard cock pressed against her back, and the image of that thick length sliding into her pussy flashed through her mind.

Her tissues pulsed with heat. Pleasant warmth suffused every inch of her body, from the soles of her feet to the top of her scalp.

Her hands burned with the need to touch him. To feel his slick skin gliding beneath her fingertips. But as she reached behind her, he caught her wrists and jerked them together to clench them in one steel-fisted grip.

"Don't move unless I tell you," he murmured in her

ear.

She gasped, nodded, secretly thrilled with the game they were playing. He was her captor, a fierce warrior, commanding her every move. She was the maiden. Most definitely in distress, but not the kind you'd read about in a fairytale.

He placed her wrists on her buttocks, tapping them. Then, he released them, and she left them where he'd placed them, understanding his cue.

"Turn and face me, sweet Keri."

She turned, the water once again pounding on her back. Now facing him, she admired every inch of skin she saw. She'd thought it before, but wow, a man couldn't be more perfectly formed, beautifully proportioned than this one. Despite the old scar and the new cuts and bruises he'd acquired fighting her killer, he was a living, breathing work of art. And as someone who appreciated art in its many forms, she couldn't help but become totally mesmerized by the sight.

Those shoulders.

That stomach!

His legs.

Butt. Mmmm.

He scooped up the soap. "Your hands."

She held them in front of her.

"Palms up."

She flipped them over, and he placed the soap in her palm.

"Wash me."

She gazed down at the blue bar, then at the expanse of smooth skin and smiled. What a treat! But where to begin.

Undecided, she glanced at his face.

With his eyes, he indicated lower.

His chest then? She reached, but he stopped her. "No."

Ooooh. His cock? She reached, but he stopped her again, "No, Keri. Lower. Get on your knees. Wash my feet." He braced his hands against the walls and lifted one foot about six inches into the air.

She lowered herself to her knees, positioning herself so the water was beating her on the back, and lathered her hands. The crisp scent of the soap filled the enclosed area as she smoothed her hands over his foot, working the bubbles along the sole, over the toes, around the heel.

It was a bizarre experience. Humbling and yet sensual too.

Intimate.

She'd never thought about it before—how infrequently one comes in contact with other people's feet. She couldn't recall the last time she had.

If anyone had told her a week ago she'd be kneeling in a shower, washing a man's feet, she would have laughed. Strange, the twists and turns her life had taken.

When she finished both his feet, she glanced up to gauge his reaction. He had his head thrown back, and fat droplets of water fell from his hair. More water streamed down his chest, the water from the showerhead falling in big drops, striking his skin and bursting into zillions of smaller droplets.

As she watched, caught up in the moment, he lifted his head to glance down at her. "More."

The words, *yes master*, popped into her head, but she didn't utter them. She wasn't a submissive, and he wasn't a Dom. They were just two people enjoying a short time together, sharing an experience she knew she'd never forget. She hoped he wouldn't either.

She went for the soap again, worked up a thick, fragrant lather then washed his ankles, calves, knees, thighs. While she worked, she noticed everything about the parts she was touching. His legs were smooth, shaven like a swimmer or bodybuilder. She hadn't noticed that before. His calves had the most amazing definition when he flexed his foot. He had a scar on one knee, a deep red, jagged line that ran diagonally across the front. His thighs were also strong, defined, heavily muscled. And the insides were extremely sensitive. He flinched when she touched him there, and his cock jumped. He groaned, and the sound vibrated through her body like an electrical charge.

"Don't stop," he demanded.

More soap.

Now, she was at his testicles. She touched them shyly at first, unsure whether he wanted her to go there yet or not. He didn't stop her, so she grew bolder, massaging them with her soapy hands, cupping them, weighing them. She slipped her fingertips between his ass cheeks, smoothing some soap around his anus then resoaped her hands and went for his cock.

He stopped her this time. "No."

Party pooper.

She gave him a playful pout but he simply shook his head.

"More," he demanded again.

She went back to work, washing his glorious stomach—picture-perfect washboard abs—his lean hips and perfectly rounded butt, his strong back, chest and shoulders. Arms that bulged with heavy muscle when he flexed, hands that performed magic on her body with every stroke. Neck. Hair—shaggy layers that framed his face. So sexy. So perfect.

He closed his eyes as she worked some lavender-scented shampoo into his hair. She kissed his nose. His cheek. His long eyelashes. Finally, he rinsed. Smiled. Took the soap from her, scrubbed it between his hands and reached for his cock.

She watched, shamelessly captivated, as he stroked his length, the soap lubricating his hands. Up and down, slowly, his fingers curling over the head before moving to the base again. Finally, he gently pushed past her and rinsed off, head to toe.

Stepping out of the spray, he motioned to her. "Now it's your turn."

Oooh, was he going to wash her? How fun! "Okay."

She closed her eyes, widened her stance when he nudged her ankles, and let her head fall back as he explored every single inch of her body. Breasts. Armpits. Neck. Stomach. Legs. Pussy. He lathered her slowly, meticulously, caressing her all over, not missing an inch. She had never been so thoroughly touched. Felt so pampered. Ached for release so badly.

"I want you," she admitted when he stopped. She blinked open her eyes as he directed her into the spray, ran his hands over her breasts, pressed his hard body against her back. Her head dropped back again, this time resting on his strong chest, and she groaned. Such ecstasy. Such frustration.

He reached around her and cut off the water, and dazed, she staggered out of the enclosure, swiping a towel off the counter. Behind her, she heard Talen get out as well, and she grabbed a towel for him, twisting to hand it to him over her shoulder.

"Thank you." Instead of taking the towel from her, he grabbed her wrist and yanked, and she stumbled around, tumbling into his arms with a surprised squeal.

He caught her up in his arms, scooping her off her feet, and carted her out of the bathroom. A quick right, and they were in the spare bedroom. A single heartbeat later she was bouncing on the bed, on her back, looking up at a man who was clearly ready to gobble her up.

She was most definitely game to be gobbled.

In fact, if he didn't pounce upon her and take her right this minute, she was going to do something desperate. Yes, a hot shower tended to warm her up, but that shower had done a lot more warming than any had before.

Thankfully, he did exactly what she hoped. No fooling around. He settled between her spread legs and thrust deep inside her, and oh it was heaven to have him filling her at last.

Beneath him, she let her heavy eyelids fall closed and concentrated on the wonderful sensations playing through her body. The glorious friction deep within her as he slowly glided in and out of her tight sheath. The thrumming beat pounding in her chest. The tingly burn that followed his every touch, stroke, caress. The taste of him in her mouth as she opened her lips to let his tongue inside. His lovemaking was a complete claiming. He took and took and took, and she willingly gave and gave and gave, allowing him to possess her as thoroughly as he wished.

Their fucking started at a slow, languid pace but quickly changed. His thrusts came faster, his movements sharper, harder. His touches firmer. Strokes became grabs, pinches, taps. Kisses became nips, bites, hard suckles.

But her body rejoiced in the change as it carried her away, to a magical place where sensations blended until she could no longer tell one from another, until her body was tight, trembling, on the verge of tumbling over the crest of a mighty mountain.

"Let me fuck you," Talen whispered, slamming into

her pussy one final time before withdrawing. "Here." His finger slipped into her anus, stretching the tight ring of muscles.

A pulse of feverish wanting throbbed through her. "Yes."

She'd never let a man take her there. Never had even imagined doing so. But now she couldn't *not* do it. He wanted it, and she wanted what he did. It was as if their minds, their souls, and not just their bodies, were joined as one.

He helped her over onto her stomach, dragged some pillows to prop her upper body up, grasped her hips and spread some of her juices over her anus. "I'll go slowly, and I'll stop if you tell me."

"Okay." A shudder swept through her body. She clamped her eyes closed and concentrated on relaxing from the waist down.

Burning. Pain. She couldn't help tightening. It was a reflex.

"You need to relax."

Easy for him to say.

"If you can't, think about pushing against me, rather than keeping me out."

Push against. That might work. She clamped her eyes closed and concentrated, applying gentle pressure out as he pressed to gain entry and slowly, she felt her muscles open. The head of his cock slipped inside.

She gasped but didn't ease up.

"Yes." His voice was a deep growl. Throaty. Sexy. His fingertips dug into the soft flesh of her hips. "Oh yes." He pushed gently, and slowly more of him inched inside her, filling her. "Touch your pussy."

Now trembling and on the verge of either passing out from sensation overload or exploding from a supersonic orgasm like none she'd ever experienced, she reached between her legs, found her clit and began circling over it with an index finger moistened with her own juices.

He sank in deeper.

Her clit was throbbing, the most amazing pulses of heat rippling out from her center, spreading.

Ohhh, that felt amazing.

"Yes, that's it. Damn, you're so beautiful. I can't get enough. I don't think I could ever get enough, even if I could have you every night for centuries."

Every night. For centuries. That sounded like heaven right now.

"You're going to come for me. I want to feel your ass squeeze my cock."

Yes, she was going to come. For him? Even better, that it was for him. More thrilling. Sexier.

"Come for me," he demanded, raw desperation plain in his deep voice.

She increased the pressure to her clit, reached her other hand down—leaving her upper body supported by pillows—and curled two fingers into her pussy.

Hot.

Pulsing.

So close. Almost.

He eased his cock back, until it was not quite out then slowly pushed it back inside. Delicious friction.

A gush of hot juices coated her fingers, and the walls of her pussy clamped around them. She stroked the ridged walls, finding that place where it felt soooo good. More circles on her clit, more strokes inside. Talen's cock glided out then back in her ass.

And an inferno swept through her body. Her clit pulsed. Her vagina spasmed around her fingers, and her anus clenched around Talen's cock.

"Yessss." He gave a low growl, backed out then thrust back inside, seating himself deep within her ass. So hard. So thick. Hot come filled her. "My Keri," he muttered and slumped down, crushing her beneath him. He kissed her neck, her earlobe, her hair. Then he eased out of her, leaving her feeling empty and shivery. Rolled her over onto her back, and lay beside her, gathering her into his arms. "Don't move." His chest rose and fell swiftly as he gulped deep breaths.

She smiled as she snuggled up to him. She flopped one leg over his, rested her head on his ribcage, listened to the loud thump of his heartbeat.

Her whole body twitched and shook. Still. And she was dragging in air to fill her depleted lungs with just as much desperation as he was. Wow. That had been...there were no words.

Mind blowing. No, too cliché.

Amazing. No, too tame.

The most wickedly decadent fuck she'd ever experienced. Would ever experience. Would ever even dream of experiencing.

That almost described it. Good thing she didn't have to.

She'd learned something about herself. That made it so much more amazing.

Talen's hand smoothed up her arm. His heartbeat was slowing, his breathing still fast but not as heavy as it had been. His scent and the smell of sex hung heavy in the air. On her skin. In her hair. Everywhere.

She wished she wouldn't have to wash it away, that she could bottle it up and save it, so that when he was gone...

She suddenly felt like someone had kicked her in the gut. She jerked upright, and he lunged forward.

"What's wrong?" he asked.

Her eyes burned. Her nose. She sniffled, dragged the back of her hand over her eyes. She wanted to tell him the truth but she knew she couldn't. Not after what had happened earlier. If she admitted she was upset about his leaving, he'd find a way to end it now, to let that killer find them, murder him, in front of her.

Nonono.

Somehow, she had to find a way to stop it. Period. Ancient gods, curses, whatever. There had to be something that could be done.

And she would find it. Or die trying.

Chapter Eleven

It was strange, spending so much time with one person like this—doing practically everything together with no break at all. There wasn't even a place, other than the bathroom, where she could go to be by herself.

Keri had always told herself she'd go bonkers if she ever found herself in such an overbearing, intense, restrictive relationship. Everyone needed space. Especially her.

So, why was she still giddy and quivery around Talen? Why wasn't she ready to shove him out the door and tell him to leave her alone for a while?

Over the hours since they'd fucked, they'd settled into a comfortable partnership. An intimacy that would take the average couple weeks to build, maybe longer. But out of necessity, it had taken them only hours.

Talen had given a full account of every historical inaccuracy in the episode of *The Tudors* they watched while eating lunch. He did the same when they watched *The Other Boleyn Girl* after that. Clearly, Talen got a real kick out of picking apart historical movies, and Keri was overwhelmed with the knowledge he'd accumulated over the centuries.

Even though she believed he was as old as he said, and had seen so many historical events with the very same eyes she now gazed into, it was still hard to believe he was truly that old. That in his lifetime he'd watched so many significant, world-altering events, witnessed firsthand so many changes. It was mind-boggling.

Later, after watching yet another historical movie that had, evidently, twisted the facts to such a degree that it was laughable, she looked at Talen and sighed.

He'd ruined *Braveheart* for her forever.

Lounging on the couch, her feet kicked up, legs resting on Talen's lap, she stretched her arms over her head. "I've never watched so many movies in a row. My butt is numb."

He squeezed her thigh. "I could massage it for you."

She giggled. Her face warmed, and a few bits of her anatomy tingled as a flurry of naughty images played through her mind. "You'd enjoy that, wouldn't you?"

"So would you. I promise."

"And I believe you." She grabbed the remote from Talen and hit the Guide button. Cable was such a wonderful thing. "What're we watching next? How about we find a contemporary movie? I'm running out of favorite historical films, thanks to you."

"Let me see what I can find." He snatched the remote out of her hand and started flipping channels, but just as he found something that looked promising, the lights flickered then cut out. The television went black.

"Why'd the lights go out?" Keri swung her legs off Talen and scooted closer to him, realizing suddenly how much safer she felt knowing he was right there, beside her. "I wonder if the whole block lost power or just us?"

"I'll check." The couch cushion shifted as Talen stood.

"How's your neck?" Keri sat in the pitch-black, her nerves twitchy, blinking at the darkness. She leaned back against the sofa, breathing fast and fighting the nausea that came with genuine terror.

"Fine. Not even a tingle." A sliver of murky light cut into the room as he pulled the drapes apart. "Those skies don't look good. I think we're in for a bad storm."

Keri shot to her feet and scrambled to the window to take a look for herself. "We lost power before the storm?" Ever since she was a kid and her house was struck by lightning, she'd had a fear of thunderstorms. Silly. Immature. Whatever. Her terror was very real. And very persistent. To this day, she hadn't been able to shake it. That was even without a killer on the hunt making things worse.

"I don't see any lights on in the neighbor's houses either." He tried to close the curtains, but Keri caught one and pulled it open again. "I can go check the circuit breakers."

"I'll go with you." Most of the time, she was able to freak out in private, with no witnesses. This time she wouldn't be so lucky. She didn't dare sit there in the dark by herself. Not with a murderer out there, somewhere, trying to track her down.

Dammit, those angry clouds looked bad. Her insides churned. Her heartbeat kicked into overdrive.

The lights blinked back on, and for a moment, she breathed a little easier. Until they cut out, again.

She wrapped her arms around herself, jerking when a brilliant bolt of lightning zinged to the ground in the distance.

Ohhh boy. They were in a house built on a concrete slab. No basement. Not a good place to be during a storm.

Was that a wall cloud over there, that black patch over the neighbor's garage?

Talen twisted, glancing over his shoulder, the wan glow from the streetlamp outside highlighting one side of his face. He frowned. "You look tense."

Trying to hide how tense she truly was, she shrugged. "Storms make me a little nervous."

"A little?" He pulled her into his arms, and she felt a smidge better. Until another bolt of blue light illuminated the sky.

A sharp clap of thunder followed a split second later, and she jerked against him, burying her face in his chest. "Hey, it doesn't help that there's a guy out there trying to kill us!"

"But he's not close by. I promise. How about we go sit down?" With one hand, he pulled the curtain closed then he gently helped her to the sofa.

She slumped onto the couch, crossing her legs and clutching a pillow in her arms. "I'm silly, I know."

"I said no such thing. There's plenty of reason to be afraid."

"Aren't we going to check the circuit breakers?" She couldn't see his features clearly, it was so dark in the room. For all she knew, he was grinning. But his voice held no hint of amusement.

"Sure."

"The service panel is in a closet off the kitchen." She stood, clawing at the dark until she caught a part of Talen. An arm. His hand found hers. This time, he led her down the hallway. Slowly, silently they crept. Every muscle in her body was tight, and she swore she didn't exhale, not once. They reached the closet without running across any armed killers, and she breathed a tiny sigh of relief.

Talen pulled the door closed behind them as they both stepped inside, shutting them into a space the size of a coffin, and dark as one too. "There should be a flashlight on the shelf up there. I'm too short to reach."

A few seconds later, a weak, yellow beam illuminated the grey cover to the circuit-breaker box. Talen opened it, pushed each button then shut it and pointed the light at the door. "No deal."

"Damn."

He used the flashlight as he led her back to the living room. Shined it on the cushion. "Lay down on your stomach. I'm going to give you that back rub to help you relax."

When another earsplitting crack of thunder made her

jump, she did as he bid, fully expecting him to rub her back for about ten seconds and then molest her—which would be just fine with her, if they weren't hiding from a killer during a bad storm.

He didn't. Instead, he cut off the flashlight, swung a leg over her, straddling her legs, and rubbed for twenty seconds, thirty, more. And it felt so freaking unbelievable she closed her eyes and moaned, despite the loud clatter of rain against the window, the eerie whistle of the wind.

He chuckled. "That good?"

"That good. I'm almost not freaking out about the storm." She made a liar of herself when she jumped at the sound of yet another loud thunderclap.

"You see? This is good. I'm glad it's storming now. I want to know about my Keri. What she is afraid of. What she wants in life. What she dreams about."

Ohhh, his hands were magic, and not just when he was touching her sexually. Miraculously, she felt her muscles softening beneath his skilled touch. "Mmmm. Fears? I think you know about most of those now. And dreams? I dream about...someday doing art for a living. Having a show at a gallery, and having people clamoring for my work."

"That sounds like a very rewarding dream."

"It would be. Sadly, I doubt it'll happen—at least while I'm alive."

"Why?"

"Well...until now, I haven't done anything to make that dream happen. I found fault with every piece.

183

Nothing was good enough. Wrong colors. Bad shading. Terrible perspective. Whatever. Always an excuse. So I never let anyone see anything I did. Not even a sketch. Until you."

"I...don't know what to say."

Things were getting too serious, too heavy. Hoping to lighten the mood, Keri added, "Hey, everyone knows artists rarely get famous until after they're dead anyway."

His soft laughter sent waves of desire rippling through her body, despite the fear still coiled through her insides. "So in the meantime, what are your hopes for the time *before* you die?"

"Oh, I don't know. I guess to someday have an art gallery of my own, sell other dead artists' work."

"Mmmm." His hands moved lower, to the backs of her thighs. "What about in your personal life? Do you want to be married? Have a family?"

"No. I've never thought of myself as the settling-down-and-getting-married kind of girl. I'm too stubborn for any man to live with for long. I scare them off pretty quickly, at least the normal ones."

"You're not too stubborn for this man."

"It hasn't been that long. Trust me, if we were dating, like regular people, I'd be driving you nuts by now. Even though you're immortal, you're still too normal for me not to. You have lived a life I can't begin to comprehend, yet you're still a man. A human being. A person with normal wants and needs and feelings."

There was a long pause, filled with the loud rattle of

rain and distant rumble of thunder, then he asked, "So why do you think it's different between us?" Now his hands moved higher, to the small of her back. His fingertips pressed deep into her knotted muscles. Ohmygod, that felt amazing.

"Because we were forced into this situation," she mumbled, semi-unconscious.

"Forced?"

"Sure." She sighed, rocking her head to the side to pull in a deep breath. "We're together because some psycho wants me dead."

"But we decided to prolong things. It could have ended—"

"By your death."

"Exactly."

"Sorry, but it's human nature to avoid death. At least it is for me. So prolonging this is pretty normal."

"Then you're only here with me because you don't want to die? And you don't want me to die?"

She didn't answer right away. Because she didn't know how to answer that question. Why was she still here with him? Was it only fear? That was a part of it, but at this stage of the game a very small one. Guilt? Perhaps that was playing a role too. "I'll plead the fifth on that one."

"You are very evasive."

"Only when you ask a question I don't want to answer."

"Uh-huh." His hands worked up her back, and she had what could only be described as a divine, out-of-body-type experience. She was in heaven. Literally. There, among God, the gods, whoever. No one could possibly be better at this than Talen. Not only were her muscles unknotting but so was her mind. Thoughts slowing. Mind settling.

Ahhhhh.

"What do you want, Keri?" he asked as he continued performing magic on her back. "What do you secretly desire, more than anything? More than being an acclaimed artist?"

"I don't know."

"You can trust me. I'll be taking your secrets to my grave."

That was not the right thing to say at the moment. "Uh, Talen..."

"What I meant, is I won't tell anyone. I won't have the opportunity. So this is your chance to let go, to unshackle yourself from those chains you've wound around yourself, and let yourself dream."

"Why do you keep asking me questions like this?" She pushed up onto her knees, wrapping her arms around herself, and stared at the shadow she knew was Talen. "It feels like you're prodding." After a beat, she added, "It's not fair. Do you realize that? Not when you are guaranteed to leave me. At any time."

"Yes. I do keep prodding, like you said. And I told myself I wouldn't ask for any intimacy. I want to keep my distance so it'll be easier on you. But I can't stop myself. I've prayed for help, but I don't know if the gods are punishing me or they've just stepped back and are letting me punish myself—"

"And me. They're punishing me too. And I didn't do anything to them." She grabbed a pillow, clutching it to her chest. "They're a bunch of sadistic bastards."

"No, they aren't sadistic. They're just. Divine. And they have reasons for letting things happen in our world."

"That's a bunch of hooey. No offense, but your gods aren't divine." She used her fingers to indicate quotations marks in the air, even though he couldn't see her. "I realize you've been trapped in some kind of reality that can't be explained, but that still doesn't convince me your prehistoric gods exist. They're myths, created by mankind to explain things that couldn't be understood any other way. Things like the changing of the seasons, the movement of the stars. The tides and storms and volcanic eruptions that took lives, destroyed homes. And curses."

He didn't respond. She gave him credit for that, since she'd basically attacked his entire belief system. She doubted she'd handle such an attack as well. But he had this way of striking a raw nerve with her, and she found herself needing to fight back, knock him off his feet before he landed another blow.

The past few hours had been like a sword fight. She'd never tried fencing, but she'd watched swordplay at the Renaissance festival. Attack, offense, retreat, defense. It was her turn to take the offense. To strike a blow.

"How about we turn the tables, shall we?" she challenged. "I'll ask you—what are your secret dreams, Talen? What do you want more than anything?"

He didn't hesitate. "To have one more chance to love. I would suffer a million deaths for the opportunity to give my love to another human being."

"You're serious?"

"Absolutely."

She wanted to laugh at the irony. A chuckle slipped from her lips. "I'm not laughing at you, per se. I find the differences between us amusing, I guess. They're so profound, it's a wonder we get along at all."

"What makes you say that?"

She smoothed her hand down the front of the pillow, still tucked against her body. "I'd die a million deaths to avoid love."

He leaned closer, and she could somewhat make out his features. She literally felt his gaze on her. "Why is that, Keri?"

"Because love makes people weak. It makes them do things they wouldn't otherwise. Things they shouldn't." She set the pillow aside, crossed her legs and wrapped her arms around her shins. "You've seen a lot in your lifetime. How many kings have fallen because of love? Warriors slain? Men, women, children destroyed?" When he didn't respond, she continued, "See? Even you can't deny it. Love is dangerous. It's lethal. Toxic."

"No, I don't agree. Love is beautiful. Healing. Redeeming."

Another chuckle bubbled up her throat. "It seems we have a difference of opinion."

"It seems."

"You won't change my mind. I've felt this way for a long time. Years."

"I won't try, then."

"Good." Once again, silence settled over them. Keri glanced at the window. There hadn't been a crack of thunder in a while. The whine of the wind had stopped too. She was feeling more like herself, and not just because the storm had died down. "Hey, I'm not letting you off the hook. I answered your question. Now it's your turn."

"Oh, damn." His exaggerated sigh was accompanied by a bit of rumbly laughter that had her feeling a little giddy. "You're such a pain in the ass. Has anyone told you that?"

"Lots of people. And I happen to think you're a pain in the butt too. Anyone tell you that?"

"Only one that I recall. But I didn't hold it against her since it was true."

She gave him a playful tap on what she figured had to be a shoulder. "What are you talking about? It still is." Strangely, she was feeling like she was in high school again, talking to the baseball player she'd had a crush on since the first day of her freshman year. Yet, she couldn't stop. The lights being out helped. Because she knew the killer wasn't close by right now, and the storm was over, she was grateful for the darkness. She could hide from that penetrating gaze of his. At times, he made her feel defenseless, like he could see all her secrets.

He nudged her back. "A fact for which I am mighty grateful."

"Grateful?"

"Sure. My nonexistent 'gods' have allowed me the chance to spend enough time with you to become a pain in the ass."

Again, she found herself laughing. "Could anyone be more of an optimist than you? Is the glass *ever* half-empty?"

Silence.

He cleared his throat. "Yes. When I'm walking down the street, passing couples holding hands, juggling squirming toddlers at the zoo, looking into each other's eyes in the park. When I pass a mother hugging a child in the grocery store. Or an elderly man sitting on his front porch, smoking a cigar with his best friend."

Such loneliness. She could hear it in his voice. Could practically feel it. A tight sensation squeezed her chest. "No family. No friends...I can't imagine how sad you must be sometimes."

Gently, he placed a hand against her face, cupping her cheek. "But that just makes this time that much sweeter. Now, with you, the world is wondrous," he whispered, his voice thick with emotion. "Colors are incredibly vivid. Scents glorious. Sounds a sweet symphony."

The lights blinked on, filling the room with muted

light and making her feel exposed and vulnerable for a split second. A man's voice cut into the silence, and Keri jerked reflexively. Her heart slammed against her breastbone. Then her gaze snapped to the source of the sound, the television.

"When you don't measure your mortality in hours, Keri, it's so easy to take things for granted. Not me. I know exactly how precious a hug from a friend or a touch from a lover is."

She met his gaze, finding genuine joy and wonder in his eyes. She was the source of those feelings? Unbelievable. "I never thought about it." She rested her hand on his and glanced around the room, the deep red curtains, the pattern in the coverlet, the hue of the walls.

"It's true. Every second I spend with you is a gift."

She hesitated, even now, after such a sweet moment of vulnerability, waging a war as she looked upon Talen. He was like no man she'd ever met. And she was absolutely certain she would never know a man like Talen again. It was sad that nobody else would either, that he'd never get the chance to love like he wished, to make some woman ridiculously happy, like she knew he could. He was attentive, eager to please and full of life. So grateful for everything. How could he not?

"I don't know what to say, Talen. We've spent mere hours together and yet..." She was not going to say that word. Not. "You're a very special guy, and if I had any pull with your gods, I'd ask them to release you from the curse so you could get that chance."

Talen let his hand fall from her face, catching her fingers in his. They landed on the couch, next to Keri's bottom. "You hesitated. What were you going to say, Keri?"

She couldn't feel what she was thinking. It was impossible. No. It was pity. Yeah. Well, maybe. She shook her head, her thoughts whipping around in her head like a flurry of leaves caught in a whirlwind. "I don't know." She gave him a tense smile, weaving her fingers between his. She stared down for a few seconds, crazy words popping into her head. "Um, I *want* to be loved too," she admitted, the confession shocking her.

She swore before today she hadn't wanted anything to do with love. Heck, she'd sworn less than a half-hour ago that she wanted nothing to do with love. She'd felt that way for years. How could she have changed her mind so suddenly?

She lifted her gaze, not sure what to expect to see.

Talen looked like he'd just taken a barefoot stroll over a pile of red-hot coals. His cheeks were flushed, his lips curled into a smile that was tense but still glorious. In his eyes, she saw something far different from pain glittering in the shadows, and that something sparked a plethora of conflicting emotions within her. Oddly, she didn't feel the one she'd expected—regret.

Wow, that was something.

She felt her face warming, and she had to do something to break the tension that seemed to be zapping between them. She scrubbed her face with her hands, eyes closed.

Darkness. Safety.

"Keri, it's okay," Talen said.

"I don't know what's happening here," she mumbled, still hiding behind her cupped hands. "You're changing everything, and I don't get that."

"I know I should apologize, but I can't get myself to do it." Gently, he pulled her fingertips away from her face, holding them like they were fragile.

Keri allowed herself to look at him, finally, and she was rewarded with a smile. It wasn't a beaming one, but it was genuine.

"I think the storm's over." He leaned closer, closer still, and she knew he was going to kiss her, and she was glad. Talking was difficult. Scary. But not kissing.

She closed her eyes, and waited. Finally, his mouth met hers. Softly, a fleeting, sweet brush across her lips. A tingle buzzed through her body, and her breath caught in her throat.

His hold on her hands firmed as his mouth brushed over hers a second, third time, fourth, fifth. His fingers curled around her wrists like steel bands.

She liked that sensation. It was a naughty thrill. Dark. Weirdly erotic. "Talen," she whispered against his mouth, her lips barely touching against his, their breath mingling, the air in the room charged with invisible electricity.

Her heart jumped in her chest when he jerked her

hands behind her back, pinning them back with one hand and capturing her face with the other. The kiss turned hard and possessive, just like his touch. His tongue pushed against the seam of her lips, slipping inside when she parted them. It caressed, explored, subdued, filled her mouth with his sweet flavor and her blood with simmering warmth.

Suddenly, she knew what she needed from Talen.

This was her chance, the one and only opportunity she might get in her life. She didn't want to let it pass, couldn't let it.

If she only had the courage to say the words...

Chapter Twelve

Talen ignored the slight tingling at his nape, instead focusing on the glorious sight before him. Once again, he marveled at how kind the gods had been. Generous, but also cruel. To bring such a lovely human being into his life, one who not only wanted what he might offer if he were free, but who needed it. Desperately. He could see now, in her eyes, the depth of her loneliness, her need.

We don't have much more time.

The thought of backing off had been banished the moment she'd said those wonderful words. It wouldn't do any good withdrawing. Not now. No. They had begun this journey together. They had both made the decision to follow this road. They would see it through.

For the first time in many, many years, he would not die with nobody but a stranger to grieve. Keri would witness his sacrifice. She would suffer with him.

He pulled her to him, encasing her small body in his arms. He pressed a palm to the side of her head and kissed her hair, inhaling deeply. She smelled wonderful, of woman and home and flowers. Life. Happiness. Sunny summer days. Those were the images that unique blend of scents inspired.

She slipped her arms around his waist and clung to him, her embrace not quite as tight as his but close. They remained that way for who knew how long. Silent. Their bodies pressed tightly together so that each subtle movement, every breath was felt by the other.

There were a lot of things he needed to say to her. Somehow he needed to find the perfect words, but he couldn't. A lump the size of a small mountain had wedged in his throat. Instead, he let his body communicate what his words could not. How deeply he appreciated her confession. How much he respected her. How miserable he was, knowing all memories of her would be erased the moment he died. And how beautiful he thought she was, deserving of the one thing she seemed to be most afraid to seek—love.

His hands explored her neck, shoulders, face as he buried his nose in her fragrant hair and closed his eyes. He longed to burn the memory of every sensation into his mind, but when he died his body would surrender them. The smells. The tastes. The sights. It was a cruel truth, but it was the only reality he had known for a very long time. The moment he breathed his last breath in this life, the memories of Keri would slip from his grasp, blurring into vague, shadowed images in his mind. All but lost. Just as his memories of every other victim had. All but one, Tanith.

He felt his body heating, his self-control slipping away. His blood burned. His muscles pulled taut. A pounding need radiated out from his center, spreading up his torso and making him breathless. His touches grew firmer, possessive, and Keri responded, arching her back to press against him, mewling softly, parting her lips and letting her head fall back.

He nibbled a line down one side of her face, nipping an earlobe as he passed, following the thrumming pulse lying below the petal-soft skin of her neck, the rigid line of her collarbone.

He yanked on her clothing, desperate to feel her skin, to taste her everywhere. She surrendered with a sigh, lifting her arms to let him pull her shirt over her head. Her bra came next, and her full breasts bounced free, the succulent pink tips rigid temptation. He lifted one full globe and bent to take her nipple into his mouth.

Sweet heaven.

He suckled, licked, nipped until he had his fill and she was trembling and swaying before him. Then he gently forced her down onto her back.

Damn, what a sight.

He was torn between the need to taste the other nipple and the desire to see the rest of her unclothed. Impatience pulsed through him, like burning acid, making it impossible to think clearly.

Driven by instinct, he yanked her pants down, fingernails grazing her legs. He watched as her skin dimpled with goose bumps. He glanced at her face, witnessing an expression of pure, raw carnal need. Answering it, he ripped her panties off, grabbed her ankles and pulled them apart, forcing her to bend her legs and spread them wide for him.

The delicate folds of her pussy opened, their rippled edges glistening with her juices.

The need pounding through his body amped up to almost painful levels. He wasted no time undressing, just jammed down his pants, freeing his rigid cock, wedged his hips between her parted legs and plowed into her with one long, hard stroke. His cock was instantly encased in slick, tight heat and a guttural groan rumbled in his chest. He forced himself to stay still for a handful of heartbeats, to allow Keri to adjust to his girth, and when he felt her inner muscles relaxing, he settled into a slow pace of thrusts, one that he hoped wouldn't drive him to the edge too quickly.

Beneath him, Keri lay on her back on the couch, eyes closed, her lips parted slightly and pulled into a pouting smile. So lovely, his Keri. His. Keri.

His fever spiked hotter still. Inside his head, two words echoed over and over, in time to his strokes. *My. Keri. My. Keri. Mine. Mine. Mine!*

He reached down to play with her breasts. He rolled her turgid nipples between his fingers and thumbs, dragged his fingernails down her softly rounded abdomen. Red stripes rose to the surface of her milky white skin, and her cheeks pinked as her pleasure increased.

Mmmm, she liked that slight edge of pain. As he'd suspected.

"You've been afraid, haven't you?" He slowed his pace because his body was responding too quickly.

"Afraid of what? The storm?" she asked, breathlessly, stretching her arms up over her head.

"Ohhh, yes. Stay like that. Don't move." He skimmed both hands down the sides of her torso. Her skin was smooth as satin. Warm. Fragrant. "No, not afraid of the storm. Afraid of other things."

"I have no idea what you're talking about." Eyes closed, she arched her back, pushing those lovely breasts into the air. She moaned as he shoved his cock deep inside her. "Oh, that feels so good."

"You like to fuck hard, don't you?" Repositioning himself over her, he caught her wrists in his fists, pinning them to the cushion. Not waiting for her response, he changed the rhythm of his thrusts, making them harder, faster.

As expected, she responded with a groan. Her body gripped his invading cock like a tight, slick fist. She trembled, her breathing growing heavy, quick. Cheeks pinking. "Oh, yes. Hard."

"And you like to feel a little vulnerable, powerless."

"Mmmm."

"You can't move your hands right now. You're completely under my control. If I want to do this, I can." He jerked his rod out of her body and she whimpered in response.

She opened her eyes. "Talen?"

"You've been afraid to tell your lovers, haven't you?" Still holding her hands, he lifted his hips, levering upright onto his knees. His shaft was hard as concrete and his body was screaming for him to bury it back in that slick, warm pussy. But he didn't. When she didn't respond, he added, "Or were you scared to even admit it to yourself?"

"I...I don't know."

"You've denied yourself so much pleasure. So much joy. All because of fear." He forced her over onto her stomach and leaned over her, so his stomach almost touched her back. "Let me show you. Stay here. Don't move."

He went in search of something to bind her hands, returning a few minutes later with several scarves to find her lying exactly where he'd left her. "Good girl. You see? This is what you need, what you crave. I wouldn't have guessed that when I first met you." He escorted her to the bedroom. The iron headboard was going to come in handy. "Maybe I should have, though." He positioned her on the bed, lying on her back on the center of the mattress, arms extended toward the headboard. He tied a scarf around one wrist, not too tight but snug enough to give some resistance. He fed the free end through the headboard's bars then pulled it down, wrapping it around her other wrist. He watched her as he worked. Her lovely face, parted lips, flushed cheeks and wide eyes told her she was aroused and nervous, both. A very pleasant combination, one that he suspected she would soon come to appreciate. "Powerful women, independent women still want to be feminine, don't they? Maybe more than most women, this kind needs to know her man is in charge when they fuck." His body burning with a pounding, aching need to take her, he slipped his hands between her knees and pushed, forcing them wide apart. Finally, he took another scarf, a black one that was semitranslucent, and tied it over her eyes, obscuring her vision.

When he was finished, he looked down at his beautiful woman, his lover and friend, and smiled to himself. It was going to take every ounce of self-control he possessed, but he was determined. By the time he was through with her, Keri would not only know what it felt like to surrender all control to a lover, but she would accept the truth. He was going to make sure the rest of her life was not shaped by fear, but courage, strength and hope.

She was tied up and blindfolded but ohmygod it felt so good, so right. His words, uttered with a deep, rumbly bedroom voice, only made the situation that much sexier. Her arms were tied to the headboard, her legs bent at the knees, scarves looped around thighs and stretched up toward the headboard too. A dark scarf was tied over her face, obscuring her vision but not blocking it out entirely.

She had never been more vulnerable and powerless, and yet she wasn't terrified. Nervous, yes. Giddy and aroused, most definitely. But she trusted Talen.

This man deserved everything he hoped for. If only she could have the chance to give it to him. *I would love him. I could love him.*

"There is a simple truth I want you to know." His warm breath tickled the side of her neck. "When you submit, you gain power."

That seemed like such an oxymoron. "How so?"

"Because by leaving yourself in my hands, you now charge me to focus solely on you and your pleasure. And as I dominate you, I must think first of your safety, your wellbeing and your desires only."

That made sense, somewhat. "But I'm still unable to move, to stop you from doing something."

"Oh no, you can stop me with one word."

"What word?"

"Rebirth." His hands skimmed down her body, a soft touch that made her skin tingle and pleasant chills race down her spine.

"Rebirth," she echoed.

"If you say that word, I will stop. Immediately. So you see, you don't need your hands. Or your eyes. Only one word." That torturous touch moved lower, down her legs before heading north again. "Such power you possess over me."

She shivered. "I see now."

He tormented her nipples with his fingers. Tongue. Teeth. And she moaned in misery. As he pinched, licked and stroked her into a fever, he whispered promises that made her tremble with anticipation.

"I am going to make you burn.

"Your body is mine. And I will worship it."

But as he moved lower, stroked her pussy, parted her nether lips and tasted her clit, those vows turned to sweet confessions.

"I want you so badly, I hurt.

"I want to love you, Keri.

"I just want you to be mine."

She wanted that too. He flicked his tongue over her clit, fingers fucking her pussy, her ass. Stretching her. Filling her. Stirring her passion like no man had before. As she became engulfed in the flames, she fought against the restraints. Her struggles made things more desperate, more energized and thrilling. She couldn't breathe. The air was too thin. Her head was spinning. So good. So right. So close to ecstasy.

"Please, Talen. Take me. Claim me," she pleaded. "I am yours. For always. In every way."

He entered her roughly, fucked her wildly, and she gripped the scarves binding her wrists in her hands and held on, grateful for every thrust. Yes, oh yes. Hard. Fast. Feral. Fingertips danced over her clit, and she soared higher. Her body tightened. Muscles pulled taut. Blood pumped hard. Burned. Throbbed. Her pussy tightened, inner muscles gripping around his invading cock. Desire burned hotter. Closer now. Almost.

Waves of tingling heat rippled out from her center. Yes. Oh yes.

"Tell me now," Talen said, voice strained. "Your body is mine to command."

"Yes, Talen."

"Then I command for you to come. Now."

As if her body could not deny Talen's command, it

catapulted her into the stratosphere. Talen was there with her, their bodies one. Their spirits joined. She whispered, "I need you. Talen. Like I've never needed another person. I love you."

They drifted back to earth and then she was back on the bed, her arms and legs still bound. Muscles twitching. Heart pounding. Breath sawing in and out of her lungs. And those words, amazing, wonderful, liberating words echoing in the room.

While Talen freed her from the bindings, she smiled as her mind cleared. Those scarves had freed her from fear. Talen's possession had liberated her heart.

That was a gift he hadn't let her refuse, and she would never be able to tell him how grateful she was. Overwhelmed with emotion, she wept, her tears falling on his chest—skin, flesh and bone that housed the most beautiful heart in the world.

Suddenly, the steady beat pounding in her ear changed. Quickened. His body tightened.

Dread turned her blood to ice.

Chapter Thirteen

It was time. To die.

Talen had struggled to come to terms with this moment since he'd first touched Keri. Finally, he was prepared to lay down his life for her. It was a gift he eagerly offered, knowing she loved him.

The burning at his nape was almost excruciating, like a branding iron had been pressed against his flesh. Still, he tried to hide the pain from her, determined to make this moment as easy on her as possible. He lifted her hand to his mouth, kissed each fingertip, his eyes locked to hers.

"It's time," she whispered.

"Yes. He has found us."

She visibly swallowed. "Okay."

He stroked the side of her face, following the contour of her cheekbone. "My heart, my soul, they are yours. Forever. And if some day the gods set me free from this curse, I will find you. Even if it's years from now. Decades. And if you will have me, I would be proud to live the rest of my life by your side."

Her eyes were filling with tears, her lips quivering slightly as she pressed them together. "I belong to you, Talen. No matter what. I love you. Like I've never loved anyone. I didn't know I could feel this way."

Once again, his heart soared to the heavens. He swept her into his arms, clutching her tightly against him. He shut his eyes and drew in long, deep breaths, nose buried in her hair.

He wouldn't forget her. Not one single detail. Not the flecks of gold in her eyes, or the flare of red in her hair, or the sweet taste of her lips. He would treasure every memory as long as he could. After death. He would fight to cling to them. "I need to tell you something before..."

"What?" She tipped her head up. Her eyes were dark with fear, and he hated having to tell her this now, when she was so terrified. Now was the time to comfort her, reassure her that she would be okay and the worst would be over soon. But he couldn't die without letting her know the truth.

He cradled her precious face in his hand, brushed a stray curl from her cheek. "With the exception of only one woman—the one who killed herself—my memories of every victim I have saved have been erased from my mind. I don't know why, but that is what has happened. I forget who they were the moment my spirit leaves this world, everything about them. I recall everything else, details about where I was, what I did, who I met. Only that one woman. It seems the gods won't let me forget about her." A tear slipped from his eye. "I want to remember you. More than anything. But if we ever meet again somewhere and it seems I don't..." He swallowed. His throat tightened. Nose and eyes burned. "Dammit."

Something passed across her face. An emotion he couldn't identify. She placed her hand on top of his and nodded. "I understand. Maybe it'll be different this time. Anything's possible, right?"

"We'll know soon." He kissed her one last time before pulling on a pair of shorts and handing her one of his shirts. She tugged it over her head and let it fall, the material skimming over her breasts, down her stomach, over her hips to stop at the top of her thighs.

The soft click of the bedroom door's latch disengaging sent a chill up his spine. He felt his body stiffen. He felt Keri's do the same thing. Felt her racing heartbeat pound against his abdomen.

"I'm scared," she whispered, her hold on him tightening.

"It'll be over quickly," he said against her head, pressing a kiss to it between every word. He tugged a blanket loose, smoothing it against her back. "And then we must hope."

"Yes, hope." She jerked away from him a split second after the door hinges creaked a warning.

The killer was in the room.

He spun around to face Keri's murderer one final time. Instantly, as if a switch had been thrown, rage pounded hot and hard through his veins. How he wanted to tear this piece of shit apart. Inflict every kind of horrific vengeance on the bastard for hunting down his sweet

Keri, scaring her, threatening her, trying to harm her. Behind him, he heard Keri suck in a gasp. He didn't dare look back.

The killer's upper lip curled slightly.

Like it always did, Talen's vision narrowed and the world seemed to shrink until only the murderer and he existed.

The bastard's eyes were dark and hollow, as soulless as the devil's. They swept up and down, scrutinizing Talen. His fingers tightened around the handle of the knife he held in one fist. The knife that would end Talen's life.

Not the most pleasant way to die but not the worst.

A slight movement drew Talen's attention back to the man's face. The killer's eyes flicked to the left. His face tightened, and he lunged forward, aiming to that side instead of toward Talen.

Why?

Talen lurched but before he could block the assailant's path, something struck him hard from behind. He felt like he was floating for a split second, then a sharp pain stabbed the back of his head.

As cool darkness swallowed him, he heard a scream.

He had failed. For the first time. Failed his Keri. Inside he howled in rage. Then he wept. Finally, as the blackness smothered him, a last thought passed through his mind. *Goodbye, my sweet goddess. I tried. I prayed...*

Knowing she was literally facing her own death, Keri threw herself at the attacker, to hell with modesty. Instinct drove her to defend herself. She pounded at the huge man with her fists and kicked her feet, her eyes never leaving the glinting blade of that menacing knife he held in his hand.

"Why?" she shouted. "Whywhywhy?"

The man shrugged his shoulders. "Because he still loves you. The bastard has to pay for what he did."

"Bastard? Who are you talking about?"

"Mark Hayward," he spat, madness and hatred burning in his eyes. "Because of him, my baby's in prison for the rest of her life." He grabbed for her again. "I'm gonna show him how it feels, to lose the woman you love."

"No. Please." Desperate, terrified, she swung her arms, moving too quickly to really see where she was throwing them. Her senses were overloaded, her body propelled into frenzied action by megadoses of adrenaline.

She'd told herself she was going to take Talen's place if that would keep him alive. He deserved to be free. He deserved to live and love, and, dammit, her life was empty and meaningless without him. But now that she was staring death in the eyeball, she just couldn't stand there and let it happen. She was too petrified.

But then the would-be murderer dashed toward Talen. Lifted his arm.

Fury snuffed out the fear. She charged forward.

The events seemed to pass in slow motion, every tiny movement taking at least a second or two. She dove toward Talen's unconscious body. The air blasted from her lungs when she landed, sprawled on her belly across him.

Then she felt the pain. In her back. Hot and cold at the same time. A flare exploded in her head and she felt like she was burning up. The agony. The torture.

Hurts. Please just stop.

How had Talen endured this so many times?

Keri felt her body softening, thoughts slowing. The pain was still there, pounding up and down her back and flashing behind her closed eyes like exploding fireworks.

End. Please. Now.

She was getting heavier. Sensations dimming. Beneath her, she felt Talen stirring. He was alive. She had saved him.

Yes. It was worth the pain.

"I love you," she whispered.

She could let go. *So tired. Just sleep...*

Goodbye, Talen. It's your turn. To live. To love. A gift for a man who gave so much to so many.

This didn't feel right. Not at all.

His head hurt. And something was lying on top of him. *What the hell?*

Then he remembered. He forced his heavy eyelids open. The killer was standing over him, his blade already covered in scarlet blood. Talen glanced down and his heart stopped.

Keri? No!

Her body was sprawled over his.

Was she alive? *Please, merciful gods. So much blood. Everywhere.*

Rage raced through him, turning his blood to bitter acid. "Kill me," he screamed, pounding at the floor with a fist. "Do it now, dammit. Right here. Before it's too late." More terrified than he'd ever been, he slipped out from beneath Keri and threw his hands into the air. "Kill me, forchristsakes!"

The attacker hesitated, but for less than a handful of seconds. Then, seeming to overcome his confusion, he lifted his arm. His eyes focused on Talen's chest.

"Yes. Do it!" Talen braced himself for the pain.

Waiting. One second. Two. Three.

Heartbeat banging.

Pulse throbbing.

Body quaking.

Once again, he was slammed to the floor.

Where was the pain?

He heard scuffling. *What? No!*

He blinked open his eyes, muscles tight, ready to propel him forward. But just as he lurched upright, the killer's blade sliced through the air and sank deep into another man's chest. A stranger.

Who was he?

Where had he come from?

And what would happen now that this stranger had taken the blow that had been meant for the Black Phoenix?

He had his answer, but Talen couldn't stomach it. He doubled over, racked by dry heaves, overwhelmed with guilt, regret and pain like none he had ever known.

Keri had no pulse. None. She wasn't breathing. She was dead.

His fault.

He threw his head back and released the emotions churning through his system in a long, throat-ripping roar.

No. Nononono!

He pulled her limp, broken body against him, cradling her gently in his arms. He'd never felt so powerless. Nor had he ever felt so desperate.

"Please," he begged, lifting her. He prayed, "I beg you, my gods. Please have mercy. Spare Keri. I come to you humbly, my lords. I will pay any price, no matter how high. Please, this humble servant knows he deserves no kindness, but Keri...sweet Keri..." His words trailed off as his throat closed up, trapping the rest of the sentence in his chest.

He sobbed, buried his face in the crook of her neck. Tears he had trapped inside for centuries burst forth, flowing from his eyes, an eternity of anguish feeding them.

If only he'd taken that first blow. Keri would be alive right now, free to go on with her life. He'd been so fucking selfish, putting her in danger as he had. Playing with the gods' patience, testing them. He'd feared punishment. And what a punishment they had delivered.

Slowly, reluctantly, he set Keri down, arranging her hair, arms, body so she looked like she was sleeping peacefully. The color was fading from her skin, making the once beautiful ivory tone flat, ashen and lifeless.

He glanced at the man who had jumped to his rescue, now lying face down. Arms were thrown over his head, elbows bent. One leg was bent as well, giving the suggestion that he had been moving forward when he'd fallen. Talen checked him for a pulse. There was none.

Something snapped inside him.

This was it. He'd had enough. There was one way he could escape this hellish curse. He had lied to Keri earlier, when she'd asked, afraid the truth would hurt her too much. If he committed suicide, he would not come back to life. The cycle would end. Granted, by taking his own life, he surrendered all hope for redemption. He would burn forever in hell.

Then again, there was no difference anymore. Not to him. Eternal fire. Eternal agony.

He pushed the man over onto his back and slowly pulled the knife out of his chest. Tears blurring his vision, he pressed the knife to his throat, prepared to face the wrath of the cruel, merciless gods.

At least this way he wouldn't be responsible for

another human being's death again.

As he pressed the blade deeper into his flesh, he stared down at the dead man, waiting for the sharp bite.

He stopped. Something wasn't right.

His gaze traveled over the man's limp body. He was sprawled awkwardly. Dressed in all black. His knit shirt was slightly bunched up, revealing the lower part of his abdomen.

There was blood spatter everywhere, but strangely none on the man.

No blood?

Talen pulled the man's shirt up. He found no blood around the wound. None on the man's clothing. What the hell? How could a human being be fatally stabbed but not bleed?

He checked the man's pulse a second time. No pulse. And although the skin was still warm, it was cooler than normal, the color gaining the pasty pallor of death. Talen had seen enough death to know it when he saw it—and to recognize something weird when he saw that too. This most definitely fell into the weird category.

He rolled the man over, checking the floor. No blood stained the carpet. He lifted the back of the man's shirt.

The tattoo.

Impossible. A chill swept through Talen's body.

There, spanning the slain man's entire back, was the mark of the phoenix. Identical to the one on Talen's own back. A mark that had been placed on him by the gods when he'd received his curse.

This man was a black phoenix? There was another? Talen had always believed he was the only one.

He gently turned the man over, settling him on his back.

The mark of the black phoenix.

No blood.

Timing that had been too precise to be by chance.

A black phoenix had been sent by the gods? To die...for him?

What did that mean? Was he free from his curse?

The killer. He'd run away after stabbing the phoenix.

Talen rushed to the door, dashed out into the hallway, around the corner, outside.

Red blinking lights illuminated the street in an eerie strobe. About fifty feet away several black police cars and an ambulance were parked in weird angles. A crowd was huddled nearby, on the sidewalk.

He didn't need to see anything else. The killer was dead. It was the way of the gods. He'd been struck by a car, slain in what would seem a freak accident.

Accidents didn't happen for no reason.

A phoenix had been slain. The killer also. What did this mean?

Was he mortal now? Was he...free? But what about Keri?

Since he'd always been the one doing the dying, he'd never known what happened to his body afterward. He ran back inside, to the bedroom, and found the man and all traces of him were gone. Vanished. Only Keri and the knife remained, the blade catching the light as he flipped on a lamp.

He turned his attention back to Keri, desperate hope making his heart race. She was still lifeless, lying where he'd left her.

Dead.

Dammit. This wasn't fair.

If he was free now, to live and love, why did he have to lose his Keri, the woman who'd given him such a precious gift? He realized he didn't want to live without her. Didn't deserve to.

He couldn't accept the redemption he'd received. Not with Keri gone.

He snatched up the knife again, but before the first cut, a sound from Keri's direction made him stop. Not sure what to think, he twisted to look at her, bending down to feel for a pulse.

Yes. Yesyesyes!

She gasped, and a pink flush suffused her skin.

Talen dropped the knife and laughed through his tears. Alive. She was alive! "Keri."

She rocked her head to the side, her lips curling slowly. A smile. She was smiling. She was alive and smiling and ohthankthegods! She was his. And he could be hers.

"Keri, do you hurt anywhere?" Frantically, he ran his

hands over her body, feeling for signs of injury. The wound in her back seemed to have healed instantly.

"No. I don't think so." She let him help her sit up, lifting her slightly glassy-eyed gaze to his. "I'm kind of dizzy. Feel funny."

"Here. Let's get you up on the bed." Without hesitating, he scooped her into his arms and carried her to the bed, lowering her gently onto the mattress. Once she was settled, he stood over her, his gaze sweeping up and down her body, watching, waiting. Was she okay? Could it be? "Do you hurt anywhere?"

She grimaced, set her hand on her nape. "Well, no. I don't hurt. But my head's fuzzy, and I had the strangest dream. It's a bit hazy, but I remember there were a bunch of guys wearing funny clothes and talking strangely. They all had an insignia on their chests. It looked like..."

Listening, he pulled the bloody shirt off her and bent to pick up the blanket. "Go ahead."

"Your tattoo?"

"What?" He straightened up, dropping the blanket. "The insignia looked like my tattoo?" Was it any coincidence that she was describing his gods? Not a chance.

"It's gone."

"What?"

"Your tattoo."

"It is?" He turned his head as far as he could, tried to get a glance of his back. When he couldn't, he quickly covered her with the blanket then hurried into the bathroom to take a look in the mirror. If the tattoo was a mark, given by the gods when he was cursed, did that mean it would vanish when the curse was lifted?

It seemed it had. There could be no other explanation.

"Talen?" she called, staggering toward him, looking as happy as he felt. "I remember now. What they said." She threw herself into his arms, tipping her head to look up at him. "They said..."

"I'm free!" He kissed her, sobs of raw joy and love tearing from his chest. "Free." He kissed her again. "Freefreefree!" And again and again and again. He leaned back, his fingertip tracing the spot where there had once been a gruesome wound. "You did this for me. I know it."

After about the hundredth kiss, Keri pulled back, smiling. "You aren't going to die?"

"No, Keri. I will." When she frowned and her eyes filled with anguish, he explained, "Just like you will die. I'm mortal. My life will end. Some day. But if the gods are as merciful as they've been this day, I won't die today or tomorrow or next week. Next month. Or next year."

"Ohthankgod." A fat tear fell onto her cheek.

Gently, he wiped it away with his thumb. "I'll spend the rest of my life thanking the gods for their blessing. And you, for your sacrifice."

Surprising him, Keri slipped from his grasp, sinking to her knees. She lifted her arms. "Thanks to you, heavenly lords, for your blessing. We will live exactly as you have commanded."

"As they commanded? What does that mean?" Talen gently helped her to her feet.

Her smile hinted at a secret. "Don't you worry about that. Just know from this point forward, I am going to make sure every day is filled with love and life and hope. Just as you've done for me."

This time it was his turn to drop to his knees. He took Keri's hand in his, stroked the back with his thumb. She was his. For the rest of his days. His to love, cherish, adore. "And I vow to fulfill every promise I made earlier. You will surrender to me. Every night. And you will feel like the most powerful, satisfied and thoroughly loved woman on the planet. We have both been reborn. I have been delivered from my curse and you..."

"From fear," Keri finished for him. She kneeled before him and placed her hand on his heart. "I won't ever be afraid. Not with you by my side. My master. My lover. My soulmate. My phoenix."

About the Author

Nothing exciting happens in Tawny Taylor's life, unless you count giving the cat a flea dip—a cat can make some fascinating sounds when immersed chin-deep in insecticide—or chasing after a houseful of upchucking kids during flu season. She doesn't travel the world or employ a staff of personal servants. She's not even built like a runway model. She's just your run-of-the-mill, pleasantly plump Detroit suburban mom and wife.

That's why she writes, for the sheer joy of it. She doesn't need to escape, mind you. Despite being run-of-the-mill, her life is wonderful. She just likes to add some...zip.

Her heroines might resemble herself, or her next-door neighbor (sorry Sue), but they are sure to be memorable (she hopes!). And her heroes—inspired by movie stars, her favorite television actors or her husband—are fully capable of delivering one hot happily-ever-after after another. Combined, the characters and plots she weaves bring countless hours of enjoyment to Tawny...and she hopes to readers too!

In the end, that's all the matters to Tawny, bringing a little bit of zip to someone else's life.

To learn more about Tawny Taylor please visit www.tawnytaylor.com. Send an email to Tawny at tawny@tawnytaylor.com.

Three nights of uninhibited kink—and you're invited.

Behind the Mask
© 2008 Tawny Taylor

Kelly Bennett is about to embark on a journey into a strange and foreign world, where men and women play erotic games of power and lust, hiding behind masks. A dark world of bondage, of domination and submission, of masters and slaves. The world of Masquerade Weekend.

But her journey is not a solitary one. She's found a willing guide in Rogan Cayne, a man who knows his way around. A man with the strength to keep her safe as she indulges in some experimentation, and maybe a game or two of cat and mouse. As she lets Rogan slowly lure her with a touch, a look, and a few whispered words, she suddenly finds she's a mouse with one very fierce cat on her tail.

Rogan isn't about to let Kelly play it safe during this weekend of decadent, carnal exploration. In fact, before the weekend draws to a close, he intends to strip away her every defense and bring the luscious little submissive to her knees.

But is he willing to pay the price to discover what lies beneath her mask?

Available now in ebook and print from Samhain Publishing.

GET IT NOW

MyBookStoreAndMore.com
GREAT EBOOKS, GREAT DEALS . . . AND MORE!

Don't wait to run to the bookstore down the street, or
waste time shopping online at one of the "big boys." Now,
all your favorite Samhain authors are all in one place—at
MyBookStoreAndMore.com. Stop by today and discover
great deals on Samhain—and a whole lot more!

Samhain
Publishing Ltd

WWW.SAMHAINPUBLISHING.COM

GREAT CHEAP FUN

Discover eBooks!

THE FASTEST WAY TO GET THE HOTTEST NAMES

Get your favorite authors on your favorite reader, long before they're out in print! Ebooks from Samhain go wherever you go, and work with whatever you carry—Palm, PDF, Mobi, and more.

Samhain Publishing Ltd